SMOKE SCREEN

"I think," Aaron said slowly, "we need a diversion. Something to pull the coppers away from the front entrance."

The doorbell rang.

"It's too late! They're at the door. You can't divert your way out of this—you'll have to surrender!"

Aaron shrugged, his arm stretched out along the back of the sofa. "In that case, we may as well make ourselves comfortable." His dark eyes rested mordantly on Amy. "Have a cigarette."

"I don't want a cigarette," she said.

"No?" The answer seemed to amuse him. "When I smoke, everybody smokes!"

There was the brief pungent odor of lighter fluid, the leap of a spark.

"Amy!" Ginny rose, screaming. "Your hair!"

Bantam Crime Line Books offers the finest in classic and modern British murder mysteries
Ask your bookseller for the books you have missed

THE STALKING LAMB

Marian Babson

BANTAM BOOKS

NEW YORK · TORONTO · LONDON · SYDNEY · AUCKLAND

*This edition contains the complete text
of the original hardcover edition.*
NOT ONE WORD HAS BEEN OMITTED.

THE STALKING LAMB

*A Bantam Book / published by arrangement with
the author*

PRINTING HISTORY
THE STALKING LAMB originally published 1974
Bantam edition / March 1990

ISBN 0-553-27171-7

Published simultaneously in the United States and Canada

---

*Bantam Books are published by Bantam Books, a division of Bantam
Doubleday Dell Publishing Group, Inc. Its trademark, consisting
of the words "Bantam Books" and the portrayal of a rooster, is
Registered in U.S. Patent and Trademark Office and in other
countries. Marca Registrada. Bantam Books, 666 Fifth Avenue,
New York, New York 10103.*

PRINTED IN THE UNITED STATES OF AMERICA

OPM   0   9   8   7   6   5   4   3   2   1

THE STALKING
LAMB

PART ONE

Chapter 1

They let her sit by the window now. Encouraged it, in fact. As they encouraged her in her needlework, exclaiming over it, admiring it, urging her to finish the pattern, although her hands were still too awkward to manage the frame properly and the blunt needle kept slipping out of the grasp of the strange puffy pink sausages which were her fingers. It was occupational therapy, and that was good in their lexicon. It conveyed to them that she was responding, taking an interest in something again, coming back to life.

They were wrong. It was just something to do while she was waiting. Waiting for the pattern to be finished. But they didn't know she knew that. They thought she believed them when they told her Aaron was dead.

Something moved in the mews below. She turned her head swiftly to focus on what had been a mere flicker at the corner of her eye. A yellow door had opened and closed quickly in the house at the end. No one had gone in or out. Perhaps the occupant had been starting out and had gone back to collect something she had forgotten. It didn't matter. A false alarm. That was all it was this time.

Her attention didn't return to her needlework, it stayed in the mews. So peaceful and charming down there, a little Georgian cul-de-sac where time might have stood still through the centuries. It hadn't, of course. There were electric lights and television aerials down there, the ringing of a telephone heard through an open window.

She liked to study the life in the mews, though. It made her feel like a scientist watching some strange species. Or an anthropologist taking mental notes on a totally alien way of life.

At other times, she liked to dream, projecting herself back into the distant past. The very distant past. It was her only escape. The recent past was a nightmare, the present unbearable. She had no future.

Staring at the pleasant red brick terrace was the nearest she could come to shutting out the world and stepping back into an earlier, more placid time. Sometimes, if she narrowed her eyes until they were nearly closed and peeped through her lashes, the young women pushing prams turned into frock-coated footmen hurrying along with a sedan chair.

Inevitably, though, that was the moment when one of the doctors or nurses would pop in. As though they had some special sixth sense that warned them when a patient was escaping from reality and might, if she tried hard enough, slip the leash of life altogether and escape them. They couldn't let her get away. If she escaped them, Aaron might escape them, too.

The yellow door opened again and the Yellow Lady hesitated in the doorway, obviously giving final orders to a sullen Scandinavian au pair who sulked in the shadows, radiating a monumental Nordic gloom. Evidently there had been another contest of wills but, as was only to be expected, the Yellow Lady had won. It was surprising how much one learned about the lives going on in the mews by just observing from the window.

Now the Yellow Lady stepped out into the mews, drawing on beige suède gloves, picking her way carefully over the cobblestones in her beige suède shoes, the folds

of her blonde mink coat rippling about her as she walked.
She wasn't really yellow, of course, more of an all-over
beige or fawn, the improbable beige-blonde of her hair
just a few shades brighter than her skin, which was wrin-
kled and sallow, with a colour that might be the result of
jaundice or the closest an English skin could return to its
natural shading after too many years of a constant tropic
sun. The blonde mink was almost always in evidence,
too—further proof of too much of a lifetime spent in the
tropics, of blood thinned beyond the power of an English
sun to warm it again.

Now the Yellow Lady was walking down the mews,
on her way to what? A bridge party? An art exhibition?
Luncheon with friends? The theatre? Something warm
and live and glamorous, surely. She was such an imperious, splendid old lady that you couldn't imagine her
life except in terms of exquisite civilization.

The thought came unbidden: *Belle might have grown
into an old lady such as that—had she been allowed to
live.*

Don't think about that! Shut it out! Wall it off! Think
about anything but that!

There was another mink in the mews—a black dia-
mond. And a full length chinchilla. Also worn by imperious old ladies, who enveloped themselves in them as
ancient knights had donned armour as protection against a
hostile world.

She liked to watch the old ladies pass by. This was an
expensive area of town, and they were not the sad defeated old ladies of poverty. These were the indomitable
ones, who had loved well and married wisely. Who had
lived through two wars, through bombing and fire, who
had survived because they had the will to survive.

*This was an expensive area of town. Who was paying
the bill for them at this private nursing home? The po-*

lice? The court? No one answered when she asked that question.

A room to herself—she knew enough to know that that wasn't guaranteed under the National Health Scheme. Yet there had been no bills forthcoming for her signature, now that she might be able to scrawl one again. Ginny could not have signed—Ginny might never be able to sign for anything again.

She hoped they weren't sending the bills home to Harriet. Their elder sister—and guardian—had problems enough of her own and no access to the Trust Fund set up for her two younger sisters. Furthermore, Harriet and Martin had enough hospital bills of their own to face. After two miscarriages, Harriet was now grimly enduring months of total bedrest, trying to ensure that her present pregnancy successfully reached full term and produced a healthy child.

Harriet had enough to worry about. That was why Amy had sent the message that she was not to attempt to fly over to them. And why she had not written again, resisting the determined cajolery of the nurses. She could not be responsible for risking another life. Later, after the baby had arrived, there would be things Harriet could do for Ginny.

There was nothing anyone could do for herself, it was too late. It was only a question of time now.

But Ginny. Poor Ginny, who was lying in another room in this vast expensive place. From which the reports on her progress—her non-progress, rather—were issued. Poor little Ginny, more a prisoner than any of them, trapped in the immovable hulk of her own body, unable to speak, unable to move. Could she still think? Remember? Did she have nightmares, too, and wake unable to scream?

Don't think about that, either!

Was that someone at the door? She stiffened expectantly, then relaxed as nothing happened. No. No, it was all right. No one was going to intrude.

They meant well. They were very kind, even though the kindness had a tingle of guilt about it, and a touch of vindication. *See*, they seemed always to be saying, *we are not like the people you have had such an unfortunate experience with. You just met the wrong people. Everyone here isn't like that. You must believe that, you must. If you want to get better.*

They meant so well, but they were so helpless—and so inept. As inept as she had been when she first landed. As gauche, as trusting, and as naïve. How could they be otherwise? They were the fortunate ones. Life hadn't taught them what it had taught her. They still believed what they were saying.

The Yellow Lady paused in her progress along the mews almost directly under the window, to speak to the young man working in the back garden of the nursing home. A pleasant young man, there every day (the best-tended back garden in London) who occasionally looked directly up at the window and grinned. He even waved sometimes—when no one was watching—uniting them in a momentary conspiracy. She knew, and he knew she knew. The grin, the wave, admitted it. Unlike the others, he seemed to disdain pretence, to realize that the shock, the horror, had not unhinged her, nor even incapacitated her mental processes. Beneath the surface apathy, she was still alive, still aware. She might try to disguise it, even from herself, but he knew.

The Yellow Lady glanced upwards briefly, just a glimpse of intense blue before the golden eyelids were lowered again. What had she been told? Certainly not the truth. The dwellers in the mews must not know—must not be disturbed, must be allowed to function in their normal ways, like some placid deep sea denizens, drifting along unmindful of the sharks slicing silently through their unheeding midst.

The girl drew back from the window, beyond the range of prying eyes. The sudden reflex action was so swift, almost violent, that it set the wooden tapestry stand rocking on its floor base. She stretched out her awkward hands to catch it as it tilted and threatened to fall.

She stared at the emerging picture unseeingly for a moment, the Gainsborough picture of a country family, the wife sitting on a bench under summer trees, the husband standing, gun swung negligently under his arm, hunting dog at his feet. Another world, another time, a long time ago, remaining only on canvas and in flakes of paint, pages of books, fragments of materials in museums, heirloom jewellery, handcrafted furniture. Safely over and done with, beyond the reach of living memory.

That was why she had let them persuade her to work on it. It was so safe, so remote—and so large. She would never finish it, but they didn't know that.

"Most people do the figures first, dear." She had begun by painstakingly filling in the background, ignoring the hinting words, the suggesting tone. *"Of course, you want to begin to get your fingers nimble again before you start on the people. You want to warm up on the background before you tackle the figures. So sensible of you, dear."* She had let them make their own deductions, invent their own excuses. They could interpret her thought processes any way they liked. It was nothing to her. She continued to work on the background: there was an expanse of sky, of grass, of trees, of distance. It would all take time, lots of time. She might not have enough time to get to the people. That was fine, even though they were remote eighteenth-century people, caught on a distant summer's day, who could pose no possible threat. She didn't want anything to do with people any more.

But . . . although the frame had stopped rocking, she

was still holding it. Now she looked at the picture closely, not concentrating on one small square at a time as she did when working on it. *The background was finished.* The people, too, were finished.

How long had she been here? Shock swept over her. *How long had they kept her cooped up in this luxurious prison? What would be their excuses if she demanded an explanation? "Under observation"? "Detained at the Queen's pleasure"? "Protective custody"?*

How much longer would they keep her here?

It didn't matter. Carefully, she rummaged through the basket of silks in her lap, selecting an off-white shade, measuring a manageable length and biting it off. She was supposed to call the nurse for the scissors, but seldom bothered. (Silly of them not to let her keep the sewing scissors. If she wanted to open a vein, she had the needles. It might be more difficult but, with enough determination, it could be done.)

The dog. She stabbed with the thread at the eye of the needle. There was still the dog to do. Her clumsy blunted fingers would not respond to the commands of her eyes and brain. The thread buckled against the needle, sliding away, refusing to thread through. She bit her lips grimly, fighting the obdurate thread, the inflexible needle. Suddenly, they capitulated, meeting and melding. She exhaled a deep breath that sounded almost like a sob. It was all right. She could do the dog.

And . . . when the dog was done? There was someone, wasn't there, who had unravelled each day's work as she finished it? Had the doctor, the nurses, noticed how far along she was? Would it be possible for her to unpick some of the background? Penelope—that was it—Penelope waiting for Ulysses.

Waiting for Aaron.

She knotted the end of the thread and inserted the needle painstakingly into the pattern. As she pulled it through the canvas, the needle slipped from her numb fingers to fall into space, swinging there at the end of the thread. She retrieved it before it fell away from the thread to the floor, and took another careful stitch. Then another.

When she looked out into the mews again, the Yellow Lady had gone. The gardener was still directly beneath the window, coaxing the long narrow strip of garden towards some improbable perfection. Already, a herbery had been created in the time since she had begun sitting by the window and the plants now sprouted leafy fronds, heedless of the advancing winter. She wondered when—if ever—he worked in the spacious area at the front of the nursing home. Or had they come to some arrangement about that? She hoped the nursing home appreciated their luck. It seemed they had drawn a policeman with a genuine feeling for a garden. It was to be hoped that they would find someone clever enough to keep it up—afterwards.

Otherwise, the mews seemed deserted of its regulars, denuded of the people who lived in it, but bristled with its now-usual quota of transients. There were salesmen, milkmen, the inevitable motorist having trouble with his car— all of them reappearing possibly a little too often to be exactly what they seemed.

And that streetsweeper, who spent so much time cleaning up and down in that Georgian cul-de-sac. (How surprised, and how very gratified, those autocratic, luxuriously befurred old ladies must be at the sudden determination of the local Council to keep their cobble-stoned street so clean.)

Except, perhaps, the Yellow Lady, who seemed a little sharper, rather more arrogant, and a bit more suspicious than the others. (She'd been around, seen something more of the world than her complacent contemporaries.) The sudden turn of her head, the swift darting of her bright eyes, bespoke that. But did she know the whole truth, or did she just have her suspicions?

Could anyone suspect the real truth?

She moved back from the window, not that it would make any difference. Aaron would know where she was, right down to the very room. He would know, too, how many police were guarding her—or trying to. Probably, it would just amuse him.

She was the bait in the trap. Tethered here by the window, while they all waited. The stake-out.

The Judas goat, who led the unsuspecting lambs into the slaughterhouse. The only one to emerge unscathed at the other side. Until the very end.

Now she was being used as the Judas goat to draw Aaron himself into the abattoir. In a way, something in her admitted the justice, the fittingness, of it.

Wasn't that the way Aaron had used her?

Chapter 2

The sun had come out as the ship sailed into Southampton Water.

"England is putting on her smiling face for you," Belle said. "I'm *so* glad."

Belle could get away with remarks like that. Amy and Ginny had exchanged amused, appreciative grins, and then turned back to the rail. In the distance, still far enough away to seem totally unreal, a toytown coast slid past them. Houses perched on miniature cliffs, tiny automobiles moved along white threads that must be roads, or perhaps highways. Occasionally, matchstick figures lifted an arm in greeting as the flagship sailed by.

It seemed impossible that a full-sized country could lie beyond those Lilliputian approaches; that, by nightfall, they would be in a city, in the centre of one of the world's great capitals.

A sensation of total unreality—of desolation, almost—swept over Amy. Surely, it couldn't be the beginning of home-sickness—not on her first trip away from home? She glanced at Ginny again and saw that Ginny felt it, too. Unnerved, she looked around at the others crowding the rail.

The clicking of cameras, the cacophony of voices, betrayed the uneasiness of people trying to impose their own image on events around them. An image they increasingly felt was dwindling as an alien unknown shore drew near to engulf them.

It cheered her slightly to realize that the others felt the same way. Most of them. There were some who stood quietly smiling, watching the coastal panorama with a peaceful satisfaction. It wasn't alien to them, it was home.

Belle was one of these. She turned from the rail with a proprietary air. "How do you like it?" she asked.

They consulted each other's eyes, and Ginny spoke. "It looks awfully small," she said.

"It is." Belle's laugh bubbled up. She was on her own territory, now it was her turn to laugh at the mistakes, the small gaucheries. "You're looking at the Isle of Wight." She waved a hand towards the landfall looming up on the far side of the ship. "That's England over there."

The flat was in a huge Victorian conglomerate on the Knightsbridge/Kensington borders. If they were not so tired from the excitement of landing and the journey, they would have been overawed. As it was, they stood in the lobby, weighed down by their luggage, and surveyed it all with a detachment that passed for keeping their cool.

"Over here—" Belle led them past a leather-covered hall porter's chair and into an elaborate ironwork cage which must be the elevator.

"We're on the fourth floor—" Belle pushed the button.

"Wait a minute," Ginny said. "The doors aren't shut tight." She tugged at them.

"That's all right," Belle said. "Actually they needn't be shut at all. The lift will still work."

"Isn't that awfully dangerous?" Ginny asked. "An elevator shouldn't move while the doors are open—and the doors shouldn't be able to open when the elevator's moving."

"You Americans are so safety-conscious." Belle was amused. "It's all right if you're careful—why, my cousins and I used to play with it on rainy days. Mind you, we were careful not to let Gran'mère catch us. And, anyway, over here it's called a lift."

"I don't know—" Ginny refused to be diverted. "I still think it's awfully dangerous."

"This is nothing," Belle assured her. "Wait until we have our week in Paris and you see some of those *ascenseurs*—they're really hair-raising."

"This is bad enough for me, thanks." Ginny watched dubiously as the lift, slowly but inexorably, moved upwards and jarred to a halt.

"Here we are," Belle said, opening the door. "Home!"

They'd known, in a vague way, that Belle came from money—but not how much. Reflected as dark enchanted shadows in the depths of the great gilt-framed pier-glass above the console-table, they watched Belle sweep across the hall, making the place her own.

"Oh, good, there's post—no, mail—no—we're in *my* country now." Belle laughed, sweeping up the handful of letters waiting in the footed silver salver beside an exquisite silver candelabrum on the console-table. Antique silver, with the glow that only generations of polishing and cherishing could give—rather like Belle herself.

"Two for you." Belle passed the red-white-and-blue airmail envelopes to Ginny. "One for Amy—and the rest, I'm afraid, for me." The rest seemed to be mostly local. Only two were airmail and Belle tossed them down to spill carelessly across the shining surface of the console. "I'll read them later," she said, tearing open one of the local letters.

Watching her, they felt a slight pang. She was already sliding away from them, moving back smoothly into a place she had occupied before she had known them. Was this holiday, to which they had looked forward so eagerly, merely going to be a long-drawn-out process of saying goodbye to her? Already, they were beginning to feel superfluous. She had obviously forgotten their presence as she skimmed through her letters, smiling to herself.

"Darling Sybilla!" Tossing away the last letter, she laughed aloud and came back to them. "Honestly, there's no one like Gran'mère. She takes care of everything. 'Look in the drawing-room,' she says. Come on—" her voice held the lilt of a child's on Christmas morning— "let's look in the drawing-room!"

Belle swept them down the corridor with her and flung open double doors near the end. Champagne in an ice bucket. A roaring fire. A cold collation.

"Darling Sybilla!" Belle said again. "I must ring up and thank her instantly. You'll be all right—?" Halfway out of the room, she turned. "You're not starving, or anything, I mean? Do start, if you like. I'll only be a minute. I'll ring her from my room." Barely waiting for their assurances that they could manage by themselves for a few minutes, she left them.

"Well, well, well," Ginny said, unbuttoning her raincoat. "Where's Jeeves, do you think? Wasn't it a bit remiss of him not to have greeted Our Miss Belle at the door?"

"He's probably up in York at the manor house, taking care of darling Gran'mère Sybilla." Amy slipped into Ginny's mood and grinned at her. "After all, Our Miss Belle will be going up there first thing in the morning. His place is up there. He's too good to waste on a couple of visiting school friends. At the same time—" she took another look around—"whoever has been taking care of things here hasn't done too badly by us."

"I'll say they haven't." Ginny began a slow perambulation of the room, coming back in front of the fire and shrugging out of her coat. "This is what it means, isn't it?" she asked.

"This is what it really means. You and I have always known what it is to have enough money, but this is the difference between enough money and real wealth." Ginny stared reflectively at the farther wall. "It's having a Lely, not because it's a Lely or a good investment, but because it's a picture of dear old great-great-great-great-somebody-or-other, and Lely just happened to be the fashionable one to go to at the time she wanted her portrait painted."

"This is the difference," Amy agreed, longing to pick up at least one of the china figures parading along the mantelpiece and see if they really did have the Chelsea red anchor on them—probably bought while still warm from the kiln. She didn't quite dare, however. Belle would be back at any moment, and she didn't want to be caught acting like a crass American tourist.

She took off her rain/shine coat ("double-duty for the discerning traveller") and laid it carefully over the back of the sofa, beside Ginny's. The synthetic materials looked cheap and shoddy atop the lush brocade upholstery—yet they had been expensive coats, widely advertised in the glossiest magazines. (Or had it been the advertising they had been paying for, rather than anything that had gone into the coats?) A sudden disquiet shook her, as though she might be starting to change in some subtle way she was unaware of, as yet. When Belle came back, she'd ask about things like coathangers and closets—even in a place like this, there must be concessions to the mechanics of living. The uneasy suspicion remained that even that would not pull things back on to a level she had hitherto regarded as normal and customary. Customs change—sometimes more quickly than one can realize.

She turned to Ginny, looking for the familiar and the reassuring, but Ginny was looking back at her with a strange and unfamiliar expression—as though she were straining to see something that was not quite there. Then, catching her eye, Ginny shrugged and laughed.

"I just had the oddest feeling for a minute," Ginny said. "You know—sort of, 'See Naples and die'; see London—and—"

"She hasn't changed a bit!" Belle burst back into the room. "I don't know why I should have expected her to. Except that, when one has been away for two years, and so many things seem to have happened, it seems as though every*thing* and every*one* must be different."

"That's just because you've been living so much," Ginny said. "Your grandmother won't change because she's done all her living, she's set in her mould now. You're still fluid."

"You make me sound like a sloppy jelly!" Belle shuddered, then laughed again. "You're right about Gran'mère's having lived—though I'm not sure you ought to put it in the past tense—"

"You mean, 'There's life in the old girl yet'?" Amy felt she had to make some contribution to the conversation, perhaps to shake off the uneasy feeling that would not leave her—or to keep the others from noticing it.

"And then some! Gran'mère's indestructible, you know. If a Japanese prison camp couldn't finish her—and she was no spring chicken then—nothing could! I'm not sure anything about her would surprise me. Not even if she suddenly sprang a fourth husband on us all!"

"You're bragging again," Ginny said, but her grin was tolerant. They'd brag, too, if they possessed a forebear like that. Their grandmothers had been pleasant placid women who played bridge, watched television, enjoyed morning coffee klatches. All very well but, you had to admit it, ordinary.

The exploits of Gran'mère Sybilla had become almost legendary in their circle. They loved hearing about her, marvelled that she could have turned out a late offspring as dull and colourless as Belle's mother, but secretly bet that Belle would turn into something special before too many more years went past. Greatness often skipped a generation, didn't it?

"Oh, I *wish* you'd change your minds and come up to

York with me," Belle said. "Why don't you? Gran'mère
would love to have you—it wouldn't be any trouble at all.
Come and get the train with me in the morning. *Do!*"
Briefly tempted, Amy and Ginny exchanged glances again
and tacitly decided to stand by their original decision.
Legends, like conflagrations, were best viewed from a
distance.

"We've got too much sightseeing to do," Ginny said
firmly. "It's all right for you to be blasé about it, it's your
country, but this is our first visit, remember—and we want
to see everything that's going."

"I know," Belle admitted. "A month isn't very long.
You'll hardly have scratched the surface of London in that
time, let alone done any day trips. I suppose you're right."

They nodded doubtful agreement. A month seemed
for ever, especially the first two weeks of it, without Belle
around. But they were going to have to get used to Belle's
not being around. After their close companionship through
the last two years of high school, their ways were inevitably parting. She and Ginny would go on to the state
college for the next four years, but not Belle. ("We always
go to Cambridge.") Belle would return to their city on
holidays—at least, she would so long as her father was
British Consul in their city. But, some day, he would get a
new posting—or retire. And what then?

Some friendships lasted a lifetime. Others did not.
They could only hope that this one would. This trip, to
visit with her in her own territory, was a step in the
direction of durability—common memories which would
stretch across an ocean, encompassing both countries—
cement for the foundations of an enduring friendship.

"I wish we could just meet your grandmother," Amy
said truthfully. "Do you think she might come back to
London with you?"

"Heavens, no!" Belle laughed. "Gran'mère stays out
of London during the summer. She's perfectly happy in

York. Although she may open the house in Cambridge for me, while I'm there. Perhaps she'll come back with me—as far as Cambridge—and you can come down and meet her there and see where I'll be 'finishing my education.' "

"That would be great," Ginny said enthusiastically. This promise of action, of continuity in the near future revitalized them all. They laughed suddenly, in a childish way they had not laughed for years. "We'd love that."

"We'll drink to it, then. In Gran'mère's best champagne." Deftly, Belle released the miniature wire cage over the cork and plunked it into an ashtray. "Get the glasses ready—"

With both thumbs, she worried the cork until it surrendered suddenly, with a resounding "Plop" and zoomed across the room to rebound off the opposite wall. Belle caught the waiting napkin around its neck as the white foam spurted up, and tilted the bottle over the waiting glasses.

"We'll have a toast," she said. "We'll drink to us—and to Gran'mère—and a glorious future!"

Chapter 3

There was a quick rap before the door opened. Amy didn't look up from her needlework. *Aaron wouldn't bother to knock.*

Someone slipped inside and closed the door quickly. She still didn't look up.

"You're a fine one, I must say." Little Nurse Jellicoe sounded almost aggrieved. "Do you know you're the only patient in this whole place who never looks up when anyone comes into the room?"

She looked down into the mews, empty, deserted. The window was only open a few inches, despite the soft mildness of the early autumn afternoon. *Aaron would not come in through the door—he'd use the window.*

"They call them patients." Nurse Jellicoe was advancing into the room, coming within her restricted area of vision. Carefully, she took another stitch in the dog's tail—the dog which should have been white, but was emerging as a silvery-grey ghost hound. She must have chosen just the wrong shade of silk.

"Patients," Nurse Jellicoe repeated, coming closer. "*Im*patients, is more like it. You're the only one the word *patient* could apply to. The others are all champing at the bit to get out of here and be gone. Don't you ever want to get away?"

She looked up then, meeting Nurse Jellicoe's worried grey eyes calmly. "No," she said truthfully.

"Oh, come now." By this time, Nurse Jellicoe ought to be used to receiving the wrong answers, but she continued advancing towards the window warily, as though there might be booby traps concealed beneath the smooth shiny linoleum. "And what about your sister? Aren't you going to ask me how she is today?"

"You'll tell me anyway." That was the truth, too.

"Well," Nurse Jellicoe admitted it with a shrug. "There's no change. She's just the same, neither better nor worse."

How much worse could you get? Only dead, that was all. For Ginny, lively, vital Ginny, that might be preferable.

"You ought to go up and visit her," Nurse Jellicoe prodded. "All this time, and you haven't been to see her once."

"Has she asked for me?"

"She can't talk," Nurse Jellicoe said, "I've told you that. Can't . . . or won't. If you went up, we might find out which."

She turned away. By rights, Ginny ought never to want to see her again. She would not inflict herself on Ginny when Ginny was helpless to protest.

"An awful business . . ." Nurse Jellicoe trawled the line automatically, although she must know by this time that it would bring no response, no rush of girlish confidence. "Well . . ." With another shrug, she abandoned it. "I've just dodged in for a minute—Matron's doing the rounds with the obstetrician."

The mews was deserted now. The gardener had abandoned his post in favour of an early lunch (or could he keep watch on the mews from wherever he ate?) and only the solitary mechanic still wrestled stubbornly with the innards of his ancient automobile. Movement again caught her eye—the yellow door opening once more. This time, the sullen au pair stalked into the mews, slamming the yellow door behind her in a defiant gesture that lost something of its defiance when one knew that the mistress of the house was not within.

Strange, that the Yellow Lady would put up with such a moody unfriendly creature. You wouldn't expect it of her somehow. You'd think she'd like to surround herself with laughing happy people, you'd think—

She pulled herself up short. She had no right to form an opinion of anyone—least of all from just occasional glimpses. Perhaps the au pair was a very good worker and not so sullen as she appeared. Perhaps the Yellow Lady didn't notice servants enough to know what their temperament was.

She couldn't say. She had forfeited all right to ever decide anything about anyone, ever again. *She had no judgment.*

"That's better!" Little Nurse Jellicoe blew out a cloud of smoke with a faint frown that belied her words. Poor little Nurse Jellicoe—that *"dying for a cigarette"* routine of hers didn't hold water. Anyone could see that she wasn't really a smoker. She puffed at the cigarette, bringing her head down to it and jerking up again quickly, like a chicken pecking at stony ground.

In hospitals and nursing homes, it was usual for the nurses to escape Matron's watchful eye by ducking into the room of a friendly patient for a quick cigarette. *Was she all that friendly?* Poor Nurse Jellicoe found it hard going, she knew. In fact, she seemed to be searching for something to say right now. A really friendly patient would throw her a conversational lifeline.

Amy bent carefully over her needlework, concentrating on trying to get her stitches small and even, the way she had been taught. Strange, that she should remember that—that it should seem so important—when she had forgotten so much else of what she had been taught.

"Well . . ." Nurse Jellicoe seemed about to admit defeat, then determinedly took another puff of her cigarette and kept going. "I saw an awfully good play last night. Do you like the theatre?"

"It's all right." She closed her ears as Nurse Jellicoe launched into an enthusiastic recounting of the story.

Nurse Jellicoe was another one who seemed to have an oddly shifting character. In her case it was understandable, though. Basically, there was only one question mark hanging over Nurse Jellicoe: Was she a nurse who had been co-opted as a policewoman, or a policewoman who had been co-opted as a nurse?

Not that it mattered. If it weren't Nurse Jellicoe, it would be someone else. Someone close to her own age, to seem sympathetic and win her confidence, in the hope that she would tell more than she already had. They must think she was pretty stupid.

They had a right to. They had listened with pained incredulity as she told the little—the very little—she knew. She had not added what she had guessed. They had guessed much the same, or she would not still be here, waiting.

"You're not listening, are you?" Nurse Jellicoe asked abruptly.

"No." She looked up, faintly surprised. It was the first time Nurse Jellicoe had ever said anything so direct. It was out of character, somehow. She wondered if the mask were about to drop, the real questioning begin.

"I didn't think so. You haven't really listened to anything any of us have been saying to you since you came in here, have you?"

"No." Still caught by surprise, she looked more closely at Nurse Jellicoe, then looked away. There was something about her that was too English—too much like Belle, something in the set of the head, the hair rolled up and hidden under the stiff white cap, that triggered an uneasy quiver of response deep in Amy's consciousness. Perhaps, without that resemblance to Belle, if they had met at a different time, in a different place, they might have become friends. As it was, it was too late. Much too late. She turned back to her needlework.

"No." With a faint sigh, Nurse Jellicoe echoed her. Leaning forward, Nurse Jellicoe stubbed out her cigarette; the air of relief was unmistakable.

"Aren't you coming along well with that needlework?" The bright professional cheeriness was back in her voice. Only her eyes were cold and faintly baffled. "We'll have to get you another one, you'll be done before we know it. What would you like next? A floral motif? Another painting? A seascape?"

"I don't care." Head bent, she saw the soundless, impatient tapping of Nurse Jellicoe's foot. It was a foot that wanted to move, get away, be off to more responsive patients, but was held in check only by Nurse Jellicoe's firm sense of duty. Duty to the hospital, or to the police?

"Why don't you try to care?" Nurse Jellicoe shifted her weight, so that it was evenly distributed on both feet now, and the restless one was still. "You've got to begin making decisions again some day. You know that, don't you? Why don't you begin now? Just one simple little decision. And then another. You'd be surprised how easy it gets. We know. We've had patients like you before."

"Have you?" She raised her eyes to Nurse Jellicoe's face, throwing the well-meant lie back into it, and watched the colour flood it. There hadn't been many patients like her before in Nurse Jellicoe's young life. Probably none at all. She could hardly be called a textbook case.

"Oh yes." Nurse Jellicoe stood her ground. "For a start, you ought to stop thinking you're so unusual. You're not, you know. Plenty of girls have made fools of themselves over some—"

Amy stopped listening. The needle needed rethreading. She had come to the end of the length of silk already.

She measured another length, bit it off, moistened the end, carefully ignoring Nurse Jellicoe who stood by, waiting—almost visibly aching—to help. She could manage on her own.

"Have it your own way, then," Nurse Jellicoe said in exasperation. The white shoes moved off, hesitated, came back and then moved away again, performing some sort of indecisive minuet of their own to the tune of Nurse Jellicoe's noisy, huffy little breaths. "I ought to get back now." She didn't bother to try to sound convincing. "Matron will be looking for me. She'd have my head if she knew I was sneaking a quiet cigarette in here."

"Would she?" It was a mistake to challenge Nurse Jellicoe, it encouraged her. Perhaps she was deliberately trying to provoke a reaction. Any reaction is better than none—wasn't that the theory?

"She *would!* She's a real bitch." The eager note was back in the voice, betokening a readiness to support the impeachment with stories and lengthy anecdotes. It *had* been a mistake to allow any opening.

Carefully, she pulled the new thread into the pattern, intent solely on that, concentrating on one stitch. Then another, and another.

"Well, I *must* go now," Nurse Jellicoe said, quite as though someone had been trying to detain her. "I'll pop in again later. It's nearly time for your lunch, anyway."

The dog's tail was finished, the silken stitches sprawled out over the width of the body. You had to be more careful now, longer stitches were harder to do than shorter. The looping thread had a greater area to get tangled in.

"Why do you always sit in silence?" Nurse Jellicoe cried angrily. "You've got a lovely wireless, why don't you ever turn it on?"

She shrugged, not looking up. The shining needle dipped in and out of the material. As though from a great distance, she wondered vaguely why Nurse Jellicoe was so angry. Oh yes, in medical jargon, it would be called "withdrawal," wouldn't it? Another symptom of something it wasn't so easy to treat. Something their wonder drugs and antibiotics couldn't reach. Was that what made them so angry—an enemy they could recognize, but didn't know how to counter?

"There are lots of *super* programmes you could be listening to—if you'd only bother." As though in a fury, Nurse Jellicoe swooped on the transistor and snapped it on. "There!" she exclaimed triumphantly, as music lilted through the room. "*The Mikado*— Americans always like Gilbert and Sullivan. You can listen to that!" The door shut behind her with a firm, decisive click.

She continued sewing, with the hesitant painstaking care she had learned over the past few—Days? Weeks? Not months, surely? How long had it been?

Then the music, jingling, insistent, registered upon her consciousness, bringing recognition. She moved so quickly, trying to snap off the switch, that her awkward fingers missed the tiny switch and knocked the transistor from the window-sill to the floor.

At least the music stopped. Because the transistor was broken, or simply because the batteries had jarred loose?

It didn't matter. All that mattered was that the music had stopped. But the words she had just heard still echoed mockingly, insistently, through her mind.

"Three little maids who, all unwary—"

Chapter 4

For the next week, they had swung back and forth like a pendulum between the old and the new: Harrods to Hampton Court; Grosvenor Square to Greenwich; the British Museum to Biba's. In the evenings, the theatres of Shaftesbury Avenue and the West End enfolded them. The whole glittering panorama of tourist London claimed them and enchanted them.

Later, they assured themselves, they would go farther afield, try to get off the beaten track and meet the people. But that would be easier when they had Belle with them again, to act—not quite as interpreter, nor yet as guide, but more as partisan and ally in still-strange territory.

At the end of the week, Ginny declared hostilities.

"Not one more museum," she said, turning over and pulling the bedclothes higher around her ears. "Not before noon, anyway. We're on vacation, for Pete's sake. And *I* need rest—even if you don't. That time-lag is catching up with me, even after coming by ship. How do jet travellers stand it?"

"Come on," Amy urged. "You can sleep when we get back home. We'll be back before we know it, and this will all seem like a dream. You'll regret every moment you've wasted."

"If I don't get some sleep, I'll regret that more. Go away—go to a museum or something by yourself. You're a big girl now." With finality, Ginny shut her eyes and snuggled down under the covers. "Call me again at a decent hour—like, maybe, two p.m.—and *maybe* I'll get up. . . ."

She would cash some travellers' cheques at American Exress, she decided. Then, perhaps visit the Summer Show at the Royal Academy, and have a quick lunch somewhere before coming back to collect Ginny. Perhaps she wouldn't come back and collect her at all—that would show her! And a day by themselves might be a good idea for both of them. . . .

As might have been expected, there were long queues at every cashier's window. She eyed them thoughtfully, the trick with queues was to try to judge by the movement, rather than the length. The longest might move swiftly and bring you to the cashier far sooner than a shorter queue which might contain someone expecting a money order from home which had to be searched for and checked out.

She stepped on to the end of a likely-looking queue and hoped for the best. As usual, all the other queues immediately began to dwindle rapidly. Only her choice remained static. If she changed, however, that would be the signal for the new queue to hit a snag, while her former queue began zipping along. Better stay put.

One thing she could do to speed things along, she hunted through her shoulder bag and pulled out the thick wodge of travellers' cheques, was to sign as many as she thought she might need. She shouldn't sign before she got to the cashier's desk, she knew, but everybody was doing it and the overworked cashiers weren't going to complain too strenuously so long as her identification was her American passport.

Balancing her folder of travellers' cheques against her

bag, she signed three twenties and a ten—according to the
current rate of exchange, that should take her comfortably
through the next few days. If she wanted to buy a suit, or
presents, or anything, she could pay the store in travellers' cheques, there were plenty left. It made all the
difference when you didn't have hotel bills to consider.

She felt her arm jostled as she signed the last one and
looked up sharply. A pair of melting brown eyes looked
down into her own.

"I say," he said, "your name's Amy. I like that—"

She looked away. Where had he come from? He
hadn't been behind her in the queue earlier—she had a
distinct impression of some disgruntled Midwesterner aching to start a conversation about the shortcomings of for-
eign travel, which was why she had become so busy with
pen and travellers' cheques to begin with.

"Amy—that's a good name. Very good. Top of the
alphabet."

She turned her head farther, the mane of her waist-
length brown hair slid between them like a curtain.

"There was a song, once, too, wasn't there?" He
wouldn't be discouraged. " 'Once in love with Amy' . . ."
He whistled the first few bars. People were beginning to
look around.

"Please—" She turned to him, noticing that he *was*
rather handsome. *And* he was an Englishman. It would
really score off Ginny if she were to collect an English
boy-friend while she was off on her own. Belle might be
impressed, too.

"Amy—" He kept pace with her as the queue shuffled
along slowly. "You're at the top of the alphabet with a
name like that. So am I. My name's Aaron—with a double
'a.' That puts me ahead of you. That puts me ahead of
anybody. Unless, of course," his voice changed, "somebody named their child 'Aardvark.' That would put him

ahead of me. You don't think anyone would do that, do you?"

He actually looked worried. She couldn't help smiling. "I don't think so," she said.

"That's all right, then." He stood to one side while she collected her currency and stowed it away in her wallet, then claimed her attention again.

"Amy." He whistled the melody again. " 'Once in love with Amy' . . . I'm going to like you, Amy. Come on, let's go and have a coffee, Amy . . ."

Chapter 5

Someone had come from the Embassy to explain to her what he had quaintly called "our position in this matter." It appeared that they had none—unless it were the classic example involving a bowl of water.

"Americans who break the laws of a country are subject to the police and court procedures of that country. We cannot intervene."

No one had asked him to.

"People don't realize it," he went on defensively—as though she had broken in to protest or complain. "They think an American passport allows them to ride roughshod over all the rules—and then scream for the Embassy when they're caught."

He seemed to expect some response. She made none. Perhaps it reminded him that she hadn't screamed for the Embassy, either. Curiously, it seemed to turn him from the defensive to the offensive.

"Oh, we've seen it all, you know. At least," he amended, frowning at her, "we thought we had."

Until now, hovered in the air between them. She gave no indication that she was aware of it.

"They think they're so clever," he said bitterly. "They come over here without enough money, but with a damned guitar, thinking they can beg enough to keep them afloat.

Or else they sell their return ticket home and live off that, then expect us to finance their return trip. They lose their passports. They take illegal jobs. They smuggle in their pot and smoke it—and push it—"

The voice droned on, listing grievances which had been festering, perhaps for years, in his mean diplomatic little soul. Through it all, he managed to convey the impression that any or all of these delinquents were preferable to her.

"You come completely under the jurisdiction of English law," he concluded severely. "Completely. Do you understand?"

"Yes," she said, not adding that she would rather throw herself on their mercy than on his. The English police had seemed kinder or, at least, better able to understand how something like this could have happened. They had not prejudged her—and condemned her.

"You're content to leave it at that?" Again, he was censorious. As though he would have thought it more maidenly of her to have fought the idea, demanded the whole weight of the Embassy be flung behind her—or pleaded for an American lawyer. "You'll accept that?"

"Yes," she said. She wondered if he were going to explain again that she had no choice about it. She wanted none.

"You don't seem to care," he complained.

"I don't." Perhaps it was another of the things she had to think out in the long silences of the nights ahead. When had her feelings towards the law, the police, begun to change? When had her fashionably campus-rebellion-protest attitude disintegrated? When had they stopped being the pigs, the fuzz, and become instead the shepherds, the protectors?

Had it been when two of them caught her as she ran screaming down the corridor, flung her to the floor, and beat out the flames with their bare hands?

"As it happens, you're an extremely lucky girl," he said. "The family aren't going to prosecute." He sounded disapproving, as though he felt Belle's family were showing a lack of proper consideration by neglecting to take any opportunity for revenge, if not redress.

She didn't answer. There was no answer to that one.

"Of course—" He began shuffling papers together, replacing them in his attaché case. (Why had he even taken them out? She had not been asked to look at any of them, to sign any of them. Had he needed them as notes for some lecture he had forgotten to give her? Or did they just pertain to other aspects of the case? She wasn't the only one involved.)

"Of course, the family don't want to see you again. You would have been requested—" he twisted the knife with relish—"not to go to the funeral, had your condition left any question that you might have been able to."

There was no answer to that one, either.

He sat there waiting, watching her. What was he hoping for—tears? Hysterics? She was cheating him of some scene he had built up in his imagination. His dissatisfaction was a palpable thing.

"That's all." He snapped the latches af the slim black attaché case with finality. She was done with and shut away now, ready to be filed into some unknown category at the Embassy. His job was finished—little as there had been of it.

"Well . . ." He stood, looking down at her irresolutely. "So long as you understand the position. I'll go along now."

"Yes," she said.

He still hovered there, as though regretting that the bandages still on her hands precluded her making any movement towards shaking hands with him—a gesture he could repudiate, the better to underline how complete and how thorough was her disgrace, her alienation from the entire human race.

She already knew.

"Yes, well . . ." Unconsciously, he twisted his hands together in a washing motion. "Well . . . goodbye."

She was aware of his final hesitation in the doorway, of the long searching stare. Perhaps, even now, he still expected her to call him back, to show some reaction to what other people might consider desertion on the part of their countrymen, their country.

She did not look up.

Chapter 6

Ginny had been ironing when she returned. With all the drip-dry materials available, Ginny had still insisted on bringing three cotton blouses and two linen dresses. If she spent half her trip at the ironing-board, it served her right.

"You've been gone long enough," she greeted Amy. "I've had time enough to blow two fuses—the char fixed them. Have you ever seen any of these English fuses? You wouldn't believe them. I've seen them and I *still* don't believe them."

"How did you blow the fuses?" Amy asked practically.

"Who knows? It doesn't seem to take much. The only trouble is—" Ginny's face shadowed briefly—"I think the char is furious about it. She doesn't like us anyway."

It was true. They'd tried to be pleasant and not make extra work, but it hadn't made any difference. They were still disliked—almost hated. ("She was probably jilted by an American soldier during the war," Ginny decided, shrugging, "and so she's taking it out on us. Why worry about it? You can't win 'em all.")

Nevertheless, they worried occasionally. They wouldn't like their absent hostess to get a bad report, to think they had been unthoughtful, ungracious guests.

"She *did* fix them, though?"

"Oh yes. Huffing and puffing and grumbling all the way through. Just hope another one doesn't go or we won't be able to face her in the morning." Ginny gave her full attention to a ruffle, then looked up to ask, "Did you pick up any theatre tickets for tonight?"

"Better than that," Amy answered triumphantly. "Hurry up and finish that—we've got a double date."

"*What?*" Ginny whirled about sharply to face her, jerking the iron abruptly with her.

There was a blinding blue flash, a wisp of smoke, an acrid smell of burning.

"That's done it!" Ginny wailed. "We can never show our faces around here again. Let's move to a hotel until Belle comes back to protect us."

"It may not be that bad." Amy tried the light switch, but it didn't work. A faint cloud of smoke hung over the wall socket in the baseboard, another cloud floated upward from the iron itself.

"Oh no!" Ginny grimaced. "You weren't here before—and this is the worst yet." She moved into the hall, opened a cupboard door and stood on tiptoe to pull open a door in a small, high, metal inner cupboard. A gust of smoke swirled out at them, setting them coughing.

"We haven't set the place on fire, have we?" Amy asked, alarmed. She hadn't seen so much smoke since the last Fourth of July bonfire at the beach.

"I don't think so," Ginny said dubiously. "But it's never been this bad before."

They watched cautiously while the smoke cleared.

"It doesn't feel hot anywhere," Ginny moved her hand slowly back and forth in front of the fuse box.

"Maybe nothing desperate has happened, after all," Amy said hopefully.

"Except that the lights don't work. You'd know that was desperate enough if you'd seen the snit Mrs. Maple was in this morning."

"Perhaps if we tipped her some more—"

"Why? It hasn't done much good so far."

"No," Amy sighed, then brightened. "Maybe she doesn't have to know. The boys ought to be able to fix fuses. If we asked them, maybe they'd come back with us and help us out."

Chapter 7

The mid-day lull was over, there was movement in the mews again. The sun had come out and a crop of prams immediately blossomed outside brightly painted doors. Later, she knew, most of them would be wheeled off to the park or the High Street on the regulation afternoon stroll.

Directly beneath the window, she could hear the brisk clipping of hedge shears—the pseudo-gardener again, bolstering his impersonation by more work. There couldn't be much of that hedge left, she'd heard those shears so often.

If the window had been open wide enough, if her hands had possessed the strength to push it higher, she might have leaned out to look.

But that was the way the *thuggees* used to operate in India, wasn't it? Lure the prospective victim to lean out of the window, then a thin wire noose dropped over their head, round their neck, a quick jerk and—

"You haven't eaten a thing!" Nurse Jellicoe's accusing voice was the first indication that she had slipped silently into the room. "Now your lunch is cold and Kitchen will be furious when I bring it back to be re-heated."

"I'm not hungry."

"You'll eat just the same." Nurse Jellicoe always ignored mutiny, it was pointless to try.

"I'll eat it cold then."

"That's up to you. The nourishment is the same whether the food is hot or cold." Nurse Jellicoe pushed the tray forward and went past her to open the window and lean out, looking downwards into the mews.

Amy moved involuntarily, as though to stop her, then forced herself to lean back. It should be all right. Aaron had no interest in Nurse Jellicoe.

There was a breeze and the starched white wings of the nurse's cap fluttered like a pinned butterfly trying to escape. Carefully, Nurse Jellicoe surveyed the mews from above, her head turning slowly as she looked up and down it. Then she leaned a bit farther out and, looking directly downwards, made a slight hand signal to the gardener below. Unnoticeable, had one not been watching for it. *All's well.*

Silly of them. Some watchdogs they were. Aaron wouldn't try to sneak in the back way through the mews entrance. Aaron would come over the rooftops.

Listlessly, she picked up a forkful of food. Despite the cream sauce, it was, as she had known it would be, dry and tasteless. There had been no taste to anything for a long time now.

It didn't matter. Nurse Jellicoe would undoubtedly tell her there was just as much nourishment there, whether the food had any taste or not. In any case it wasn't the food that was at fault. In a place like this, they would have an excellent kitchen staff. No doubt the other patients enjoyed their meals immensely.

"It's such a lovely day." Nurse Jellicoe drew back into the room, lowering the window to the point it had been at before. "Are you sure you wouldn't like to go out on the sun-deck with the others? It would do you a world of good."

"No." Monosyllables were the only retreat when Nurse Jellicoe was around. She forked more food into her mouth.

Even Nurse Jellicoe wouldn't insist on answers when some-one's mouth was full.

Silently, but relentlessly, Nurse Jellicoe stood over her until the plate was nearly empty. She pushed it away with finality and Nurse Jellicoe accepted that, picking up the tray and moving towards the door with it. As always, she hesitated at the door, looking back.

Amy bent to her needlework again, with a concen-tration that precluded distraction. Why didn't Nurse Jellicoe give up? They had fought their silent little war for so long now that she must realize there was no hope of winning. Stalemate was the best either of them could achieve. Would it be a black mark on her record that 'she couldn't gain the prisoner's confidence and make her talk? (*Am I jeopardizing your nursing career? Or is it your future in law enforcement I'm ruining? Well, if I've messed you up in one, perhaps you can still turn to the other. But which is your first real love, Policewoman/Nurse Jellicoe?*)

The door closed and she waited, holding her breath in order to hear the other, hushed breathing, if it were there. The silence continued and she looked up. Nurse Jellicoe had gone, scorning the subterfuge Amy had sus-pected. She was alone and—no, not safe, just alone.

She pushed the needlework frame away—not too far away. Close enough to snatch up like a shield again, if anyone else should invade her privacy. Not much of a defence in this cloistered hothouse world, but the only one she had. That, and silence.

Below, there was a pert, cheery whistle. Automati-cally, she glanced out of the window. The "gardener" was in view, moving out into the mews itself now, with a wooden rake, raking the few brown-and-yellow leaves from the ancient uneven cobblestones of the road. But his attention wasn't on the road, he was looking up at her window. When he saw he had her attention—however momentarily—he whistled again and waved, with a cheeky grin.

She stared down at him blankly, swept by a sudden feeling of loss, of fresh realization of how far she had moved from her own world, her own generation.

He was so young. Perhaps only a few years older than herself, but young in a way that she could never be again. It was all a game to him. Cops-and-robbers, cops-and-crooks. And he was the cop, so God's in His heaven, all's right with the world.

(Was He? Was it? Go away, little boy, you bore me.)

After a moment of looking down at him expressionlessly, she looked through and beyond him. Even then, she was conscious of the instant when his grin faded, when he shrugged and returned to raking up the sere leaves.

There was movement on the far side of the mews. Furtive movement. A long thin shadow seeking the insufficient shelter of the other thin shadows, just beginning to lengthen now that the sun had passed the overhead mark.

She leaned forward, narrowing her eyes against the sun, to pick out the figure slinking down the mews like a guilty alley cat returning to home base after a night best not inquired into.

It was, as she had thought, the slatternly au pair, going back to the house with the yellow door, trying to look as though she had never left it. Or as though she had merely popped out for a moment on some urgent, necessary errand—to post a letter at the box beside the telephone kiosk at the end of the mews perhaps. No matter that she could not have it both ways, she would try. It was annoying to know that she was going to get away with it, that the Yellow Lady had not returned yet to catch the culprit sneaking in.

Amy was conscious of a brief, surprising sense of kinship with the Yellow Lady—another frail barque sailing uncharted seas with unsuspected hazards, a barque which could founder and break on the hidden rocks of another's personality. The Yellow Lady should be safe in harbour at her age, docked at the sheltered wharf of a loving family—not adrift in a gathering storm, at the mercy of a mutinous crew.

Was any age serene? Any harbour secure?

So there was pity left in her—and for an unknown person. She hadn't suspected that. She'd thought there was nothing left, nothing at all.

The au pair had gained the house—without ever stepping directly into the brilliant rays of the sun. Now she turned swiftly and surveyed the mews to make sure she was unobserved. She did not look upwards.

The gardener, head bent, continued at his task, paying no attention to anything but the elusive leaves scudding before the erratic wind.

Loitering, the au pair moved aimlessly up and down in front of the house at the end of the mews, the small elegant house which, spread across the end of the mews, turned it into a cul-de-sac. Not quite a mews cottage—surely no horses had ever been stabled therein, the lower floor was too finely-proportioned, too much of the whole—nor yet a town house, but something in between. A place to house a morganatic wife, perhaps, or a loved, but wastrel son, too inept to be cast into the hurly-burly of army, politics or church.

("It's a lovely little jewel-box of a house, isn't it?" Nurse Jellicoe had followed the direction of her eyes one day. "It belonged to a famous stage designer for a long time. They say he used to give fabulous entertainments there." Of all Nurse Jellicoe's overtures, that had come closest to succeeding. For a moment, genuine interest had stirred, questions had fluttered close to the tip of her tongue. Then she had compressed her lips firmly and turned away, back to her sheltering needlework again. The house had nothing to do with her.)

The au pair paused at the shallow window-boxes, plucking dead leaves from the dahlias and chrysanthemums, tossing the leaves carelessly into the street, heedless of the wind that blew them down towards the gardener's seeking rake. At the window nearest the door she paused longer, leaning over the window-box to push at the window, levering it upwards to the half-way point.

A final, swift, sly glance the length of the mews; a quick lithe movement, and she had projected herself up and over the window-box and through the gaping maw of the window. Only a crushed red dahlia, bobbing on a broken stem, marked her passage.

Then a hand stretched out from inside the house, plucked the tell-tale dahlia, and lowered the window. Now there was no silent evidence to testify to what had happened. The mews was unnoticing and uncaring. Everything was as it had been before. Who counted the crowded blossoms in a tumultuous autumn window-box?

But why? The au pair had her own key—Amy had often seen her using it. Had she forgotten it this time? Lost it? Or had the Yellow Lady taken it away from her, realizing that she was not really deserving of the trust a latchkey implied—or in a vain attempt to ensure that the house was not left empty when its mistress was out?

Puzzled, frowning, Amy let her gaze wander back the length of the mews and—carelessly—encounter the gardener's eyes.

"Odd. Damned odd. What do you make of that?"

Unspoken, unexpected—unwanted—the communication flared between them, as clearly as though it had been shouted aloud.

Shaken, Amy drew back from the window, still conscious of the upturned face below. She reached for her needlework with hands that were not quite steady. It took several soothing minutes of stitching before she began to admit to herself what had bothered her. Bothered her even more than the flash of sudden telepathy that told her she could still betray herself by lowering her guard, leaving herself open to human contact again.

It was something about his face: the clear smooth curve of his cheek; the bright English blue of his eyes. Like Belle's—so very English. And she didn't want to be reminded of Belle, didn't want to think of her.

But it was better than thinking of Aaron, wasn't it?

Chapter 8

They felt faintly rakish, giving the cab driver the name of a pub instead of an address. He didn't seem at all surprised and they settled back in their seat, enjoying the unfamiliar vistas rolling past outside.

"It's like TV," Ginny said, pinpointing the feeling as the taxi drew to a stop outside a florid Victorian pub. "Just like the old English movies on the Late, Late Show. Don't look now, but we're going to meet The Lavender Hill Mob and be given our Passport to Pimlico."

Amy giggled and, somehow, the mood for the evening, the mood for the next few days, was set. An air of bubbling unreality—already hovering in the atmosphere from the moment the trip had first been planned—descended upon them. They were still giggling as they paid the driver and entered the pub.

It was like walking into a stage set—that didn't help to keep their feet on the ground, either. Heads turned towards them briefly, eyes inspected them even more briefly—yet thoroughly—and the heads turned away again. A juke-box in the corner was pulsing out an American song at least ten years old. Above it, stained glass windows contrasted oddly with the juke-box itself and with a row of one-armed bandits adjacent to the box. The entire row was being operated by an intense young man whose features were nearly hidden by an abundance of long wiry hair that spilled from his head and chin like stuffing from a torn mattress. He walked up and down the row, inserting a coin into each machine and pulling the lever, then passing on to the next without pausing to see whether the machine had registered a win or not.

"Over there!" Amy nudged Ginny, indicating a corner table. "That's Aaron."

He saw them—perhaps he'd seen them the moment they came in—and raised a hand in leisurely greeting. Amy waved back and led the way to the table.

"Ginny, this is Aaron, this is my sister, Ginny."

"Is it?" His dark brown eyes glinted suddenly. "Ginny—that's short for something, isn't it? What's your real name?"

"Virginia, of course," Ginny said, her tone a bit sharper than usual. Amy recognized the signs and repressed a sigh—she'd hoped they were all going to like each other, but Ginny hadn't decided yet. Worse, she was prepared to dislike Aaron because of his abrupt questioning.

"I thought so." There was satisfaction in his voice. "That's just right. That's perfect." He raised his hand again, raised his voice, and called out, "Zlot!"

The shaggy beard demonstrated his independence by continuing to the end of the row before trotting over to the table.

"I've told you before, Aaron—" his voice was plaintive, as were the deep blue eyes unexpectedly shining out through the masses of hair—"I can't disturb the rhythm. Now I'll have to start all over again. You have to play those machines like a musical instrument—speed, confidence, rhythm—before they'll give out for you. You made me break the rhythm—"

"Forget the fruit machines," Aaron ordered. "We've got something better for you. Here—" He swung him to face the girls.

"Meet Amy, she's mine. And Ginny, she's yours. Ginny—Virginia—get it? Ginny, this is Zlot. You see? Amy and Aaron. Virginia and Zlot. We're the beginning and end of the alphabet. Isn't that great?"

"Hello, Ginny, Amy." His smile was shy and sudden, betraying vulnerable pink lips in the midst of all that hair, like an unexpected clearing in a forest. "I'm glad to meet you." He sounded it, a warmth in his voice that had not been in Aaron's.

"I said, isn't that great?" Aaron's urgency demanded an answer—or demanded attention. With a sinking feeling, Amy began to wonder if he'd been drinking solidly while waiting for them.

"Great." Zlot turned slowly to face him. "And I've just thought of something even greater. Maybe I ought to start spelling my name Zzlot—with a double 'z'— like Aaron, double 'a.' Then we'd really be the beginning and end of the alphabet."

Ginny giggled, perhaps more at the expression on Aaron's face than because what had been said was so funny.

"You needn't worry, you're low enough." Aaron was on his feet for the first time now. He wasn't very tall, Zlot might have been taller if he'd had better posture—or if he hadn't seemed to shrink as Aaron stood over him. "*Say* it."

"All right," Zlot said glibly. "I'm the end of the alphabet. And I'm not alone down there any longer." He stretched out his hand to Ginny with a conspiratorial smile. "Come and help me play the fruit machines. I'll show you my system. Some day I'm going to get a really big win with it."

"I've taught you the only system that makes real money," Aaron said. "Concentrate on that if you want to get rich quick. Anything else is just kids' stuff."

"Call it my hobby." Zlot caught Ginny's hand and pulled her away towards the fruit machines, still giggling.

"Everyone ought to have a hobby to help them relax. One wouldn't do you any harm."

"I can relax," Aaron said, but he was talking to Zlot's back. He shrugged and turned to Amy. "Sit down, Amy. I'll get you a drink."

"Oh, I don't think—"

"Cider," he said firmly. "You'll like cider."

"All right." She was relieved, slightly put out. He might have suggested something more interesting than that.

He nodded and walked over to the bar. Ginny and Zlot were working the row of slot machines in leapfrog fashion, each taking alternate machines at an ever increasing pace. Ginny's giggle bubbled constantly and Zlot's great bush of hair seemed to be bouncing as he dodged madly around Ginny to fling his coin into the next machine. They nearly collided, and caught each other, swinging round in a wild travesty of a waltz step before breaking free.

"The rhythm—don't break the rhythm!" Zlot cried, and Ginny's full-throated laughter rang out as she met the challenge, stumbling to her next machine, catching herself in time before falling, hurling her coin into it and pulling the lever hysterically.

The other habitués of the pub were beginning to laugh, too, and call out encouragement to them. The entire atmosphere of the place seemed to have lightened. Even Aaron, when he turned away from the bar, carefully carrying their drinks, was smiling with this morning's charm.

Her last moment of disquiet slid away. There was always a momentary awkwardness when meeting new acquaintances again—sometimes even with old friends. She had been silly to let it upset her. Or had part of it been a reflection of Ginny's initial reaction to Aaron? And that, too, was probably just another shading of awkwardness, because Ginny was all right now and seemed to be enjoying herself. As Aaron walked past, Ginny even smiled at him and called out something she was too far away to hear, but to which Aaron replied pleasantly, without breaking stride.

"Here we are." Expertly he set the mugs on the table and disentangled his fingers from the handles without spilling any of the contents. He pushed one towards her. "There's yours. Drink up—we won't wait for the gamblers, they can have theirs when they're ready."

"You don't gamble then?" It was something else she was prepared to like about him.

"I don't gamble," he affirmed, the full charm of his smile focused and beamed at her. "I only act on certainties."

There was a sudden loud ringing from the row of fruit machines, a clatter of coins down a metal chute, triumphant shouts from Zlot and Ginny. "Jackpot! Jackpot! . . . There goes another! Jackpot! We've done it!" They scurried madly from machine to machine, catching at fistfuls of coins overflowing the pay chutes. Their laughter rocketed as they tried to hold on to the coins, scampering after the ones rolling along the floor.

"Come on—" Amy set her cider down. "Let's go help them. They're getting more than they can handle."

"Kids' stuff!" But he went with her, smiling indulgently as she joined the fray. He didn't stoop himself, just put out his foot to stop the bouncing, rolling coins so that the others could gather them up.

Others had joined them in scrabbling for the coins, a spirit of camaraderie animating the entire pub. With scrupulous honesty, the coins were heaped in little piles on the ledges of the machines, jokes and laughter accompanying the search for coins which had rolled into unlikely places.

Amy straightened up, sweeping back her hair and laughing. The handful of unfamiliar coins felt like play money in some child's game. "I think we've got it all," she said.

"Make sure." Ginny looked around earnestly. "I've never won anything before in my life. We don't want to miss any."

"It's all here." Zlot was tipping the piles of coins into a grubby handkerchief, knotted at the corners to form an impromptu sack.

They trooped back to their table, acknowledging the glasses raised in salute as they passed, still shaken by spasmodic triumphant laughter.

"That was fun!" Ginny sank into a chair and, raising her clenched hand above the table, let a torrent of coins fall from it.

"*Three machines*— three at once," Zlot gloated. "Did you see that, Aaron? I've never had more than two pay off for me before."

"I've never won anything before," Ginny said again. "Not in my whole entire life—until now."

"You hear that, Aaron?" Zlot caught Aaron's eyes again. An indecipherable message passed between them. "She's on a winning streak."

"It's about time for one, isn't it?" Ginny stirred the heap of coins with her forefinger. "If you ask me, it's long overdue. But—" she looked up, grinning—"maybe it's started now."

"That's right," Zlot said. "That's right—it's started now." He looked at Aaron again. "You know," he said, "I think these girls are going to be lucky for us."

Something in the very earnestness of his voice made them all laugh. Amy and Ginny met each other's glance and were swept away in another gale of giggles. They were in a new world, a dizzy, delirious, delicious world— and they were going to be lucky for their new friends.

It didn't occur to them to wonder whether the boys were going to be lucky for them.

Chapter 9

"Open . . . close . . . open . . . close . . ." They never left her alone. Not long enough. It was simpler, usually, to do as they wished. Then, after a while, they would go away again. She opened and clenched her hand obediently.

"Mmm-hmm . . . now the other one. Open . . . close . . . open . . . close . . . Now both together . . . open . . . close . . ."

She detached her mind, humouring him, letting her muscles obey his commands. It *was* easier lately, the tendons no longer screamed in pain, the stiffness was giving way to a new flexibility—or, rather, an old flexibility she had thought she had lost for ever. But to what end?

"Mmm-hmm . . . good . . . quite good. You're coming along." He jotted down a note on the medical chart they kept outside where she couldn't see it. As though she cared enough to read it if she could. "We'll have you playing the piano in no time."

"I don't want to."

"Well. . ." He smiled, with tolerant affability. "Typing, then, or playing jackstraws, or whatever you *do* want to do."

"And then can I leave here?"

"Leave?" He looked at her, startled, and covered

quickly with vague geniality. "What do you want to leave for? Aren't they treating you well enough here? You don't want to run before you can walk, you know. You're improving, that's all. You're still a long way from being completely recovered."

She shrugged and turned her head to stare unseeingly out the window. It had been a test, that was all, and the doctor had failed it. More important, he had confirmed her own diagnosis of the situation. She was a prisoner here. They were not going to let her get away.

"You keep on with your exercises." He stood, frowning down at her with a portentousness that did not entirely cover his uneasiness. He knew he had given away more than he should have. It wasn't his fault, doctors were trained for healing, not for espionage—nor yet for cops-and-robbers.

"Nurse tells me you won't even leave your room—so what would you do if we wanted you to leave here—sent you outside?" Trying to cover his gaffe, he blustered at her and made it worse. "No . . . no . . . you've a long way to go before you can think of leaving here."

He meant well, they all did. Perhaps that was his way of being kind. Perhaps when she left here her next room would be a prison cell. Perhaps they were just waiting until she was well enough to stand trial.

"Don't you worry," he said inanely. Why should she worry? What worse could happen to her? Aaron would find her, finish the job he had started, and it would all be over. She had nothing to worry about.

"You'll be all right," he insisted, and then seemed to listen to the peculiar urgency of his own insistence. "If you want to leave," he said, "why don't you start by leaving this room first? Just half an hour or so at a time. Join the other patients in the solarium. Or go down to the library—it's quiet there. But get out and about a bit. Mix

with people again. You mustn't . . . immure . . . yourself
in here."

She turned back to him and, before her clear steady
gaze, he faltered, unable to keep up the pretence that she
was just another patient who needed taking out of herself.

"It's true!" He took refuge in a spurious anger, sliding
his gaze away from hers. "Medical science can only do
just so much—you've got to do the rest yourself."

"I've done enough already," she said, and watched
him flounder for an answer. At least he didn't try to
pretend that he didn't know what she was talking about.
Give them their due, none of the staff had tried to cushion
her that much. Or was it simply that they couldn't? They
hadn't had many patients attended by a policeman waiting
for the first return to consciousness.

"Mmm-hmm . . ." He made another notation on the
chart—or pretended to—then gave a perfunctory professional smile. "Well, do as much as you can," he said.
"I'll look in on you again tomorrow."

There was a briskness in his step as he exited. All the
medical staff seemed to acquire fresh jauntiness at the
prospect of release from her company. Was she such heavy
going, or was it a measure of their true feelings towards her?

It didn't matter.

He'd left the door ajar. That mattered.

The few seconds' warning she got, from the click of
the turning knob to the moment when the door actually
swung open, were vital to her. She needed that brief
allotment of time in order to compose herself to face
whatever might be coming through that door.

She slid forward to the edge of the chair, moving
carefully because she had to rest her weight on the arms of
the chair, pushing against the still-sensitive palms of her
damaged hands as she did so. She winced, more with the
memory of remembered pain than because the pressure
was actively painful any more, and stood up.

It was curious how reluctant she was to use her legs, to do much walking—was it some sort of unconscious sympathetic link with Ginny? Slowly, she crossed to the door and closed it, leaning against it and breathing hard, as though she had run a race to get to it. Perhaps she had.

Outside that door was the hospital corridor leading to other rooms, leading to stairs, leading to Ginny—if she ever found enough courage to go along that corridor, seek out Ginny's room and face her again.

She didn't want to face anyone again—not even herself. She turned her head away passing the mirror, but not quite quickly enough. She still caught a glimpse of that ghost-figure gliding past.

They had told her that there wouldn't be any lasting scars. Within the limitations of their statement she believed them. No physical scars, they meant. The mental ones wouldn't show.

The one that manifested itself physically wouldn't be open to interpretation by strangers. She would never wear her hair long again. Lots of girls didn't have long hair, they found it cumbersome, a bother to care for. No one would ever think anything about her keeping her hair short. It wasn't the ordinary kind of scar.

Instinctively, she raised her hand to her head, feeling the short thick tendrils. It was growing in curly, and growing well. In just this space of time—it didn't seem long, but she hadn't been keeping track—it was nearly a uniform two inches all over her head. She would let it get just a little longer and then that was the length it must stay. Never again—

She had been away from the window too long. That thought cut across all others. Moving more swiftly, she regained her chair, taking up again her self-imposed vigil. Anyone might slip past while she was off guard. She didn't want to miss Aaron's arrival.

The mews was quiet, looking much as it always did.

No sign of anyone entering or leaving. And she hadn't been gone long enough for anyone to walk the length of the mews, had she?

The faint hollow sound of a taxi door slamming alerted her and she swivelled her head towards the entrance to the mews. Someone coming. Possibly to visit the nursing home, or possibly—

The Yellow Lady came into view, carrying a large bag stencilled with the name of one of the smarter shops. She had obviously dismissed her taxi at the entrance to the mews, beside the telephone kiosk, electing to walk the length of the mews rather than bring the taxi into the cul-de-sac and the consequent difficult manœuvring to turn around. One felt it was the thoughtful little sort of thing she would do.

The Yellow Lady moved smoothly and surely. A successful shopping expedition accomplished, ready for the next item on the social schedule. Theatre tonight, perhaps. Wearing whatever new item was in that bag. She'd had her hair set, too.

As she passed the window, once again the Yellow Lady unveiled those brilliant piercing blue eyes in a swift upward glance. But this time she didn't appear to notice that anyone was watching there. She gave the impression of being in too much of a hurry to notice.

At her own door, she fumbled impatiently in her handbag, was still fumbling when the door opened abruptly and she stepped inside. The sluttish au pair had returned home just in time. Another half an hour and her sins would have found her out.

She had got away with it this time. Not everyone was so lucky.

Amy pulled her needlework frame closer and took up her needle again, But the pattern in the frame seemed to blur as she looked at it.

Not everyone was so lucky.

Chapter 10

Belle had arrived back sooner than expected. Before they'd had time to consider all the implications of the situation and decide what to do.

They stared at each other in dismay as they heard the key turn in the lock. It could not be the char, nor could it be anyone else. It had to be one of the family—it had to be Belle.

"Surprise!!" She swept into the room laughing. "You didn't expect me yet, did you?"

"No," Amy said.

"How nice." Ginny managed a more welcoming note. If it sounded a bit flat, Belle was too preoccupied with her own affairs to notice.

"Gran'mère's decided to come down to London," she said. "In your honour. She's going to give us a party."

"She shouldn't bother," Amy said, aghast at the prospect. Especially now. "It's too much—I mean, at her—"

"Oh, Gran'mère's ageless," Belle assured them blithely. "And nothing is too much trouble for her—she's tireless, too. She'll outlive us all."

Amy and Ginny exchanged glances of mute distress. Given time, they might still be able to sort themselves out of the nightmare they had stumbled into. Even Belle's presence might not have been too serious—they could have worked around her. Or, more accurately, behind her back.

But the prospect of the imminent descent of the Dowager Sybilla was too daunting to contemplate. They had heard too much about her. There could be no secrets hidden from so worldly-wise a woman.

"Look!" As though to emphasize their thoughts, Belle held out the bouquet of yellow roses she was carrying. Their scent had already eddied out to perfume the drawing-room. "I brought them back with me. The bushes are still flourishing. Did I ever tell you—?"

She had, but they urged her to tell it again. In the first place, they had loved the story from the moment they had originally heard it. In the second place, it would postpone the evil moment when Belle turned her full attention upon them and inevitably demanded, "And what have *you* been doing?"

"Sybilla's Rose," Belle said. "Sybilla's second husband was a diplomat stationed in the Far East. They were caught out there when the Second World War broke out and interned. Separate camps, of course. They never saw each other again—he died before the war ended."

Belle was shaking the roses out, releasing them from rubber bands and confining paper. Their fragrance was beginning to seem overpowering.

"I'll get a vase," Amy said, anxious to escape for a minute. Leaving Ginny to provide the semblance of a rapt audience, she hurried into the kitchen and filled a vase with water. When she returned, Belle was still in full spate.

". . . and Gran'mère couldn't stand for that sort of thing, of course, no matter what they did to her. She organized the other women in the camp and acted as their spokesman . . ."

Jamming roses into the vase, Belle spoke more rapidly, as though to compress the story—or as though something in the atmosphere were getting through to her, beginning to play on her nerves.

". . . The commandant couldn't break her spirit. She wasn't like any woman he'd ever encountered before. She fought him on everything—and she knew enough about the rules of the Geneva Convention on the way prisoners of war should be treated to give him a real battle—but eventually he came to respect her for it. He liked her—perhaps he even loved her." Belle laughed. "Just imagine—I might have had a Japanese general for a grandfather, if things had been just a little different. I think Sybilla became quite fond of him, too."

They knew that. The yellow roses were proof of a strange mutual devotion, born in enmity and enduring in memory through the remainder of a lifetime. Amy felt a twist of envy that some women could have a life so bounded by love, so rich in affection. Some women never met a man and found out—too late—that they had met the wrong man.

And yet, there had been no lack of affection in her own life, surrounded as she had been by family and friends. Perhaps that explained the crushing sense of betrayal that had overwhelmed her at learning the truth about Aaron. Not just because of him, but because it hit at her very roots. Somewhere, sometime, something had been very wrong about all the things she had been taught. And so, she could not trust her own judgment—she *had* no judgment. The fact that she had taken up with Aaron had proved that. It was a terrifying thing to learn about oneself. It meant that you weren't safe to be trusted out in the wide world, away from a circle of friends who came vouched-for because their family had known yours for generations. You could only accept what had already been vetted for you, you weren't fit to make decisions on strangers.

"After the Japanese surrender," Belle continued, "when the prison camps were liberated—" Which was why Belle's own grandfather had been an English brigadier—when East had returned to East and West to West. "When the women were leaving, the commandant came up to Gran'mère —in front of everyone—and saluted her and gave her one perfect long-stemmed yellow rose from the bush he'd cared for all through the war."

The vase was full now, the roses crowding each other, vibrant with life, colour and fragrance. Belle stood back and looked at them fondly.

"Gran'mère kept the rose, rooted it—she always had a green thumb—and brought it back to England with her, hidden among her things.

"Now she has yellow rose bushes everywhere—in all her houses. And she still carries the plant from the original cutting around with her from house to house in a little yellow wooden tub. It's practically her trade mark. Just you wait—we'll come home some night soon and find that little yellow tub of roses in the front hall—and we'll know Gran'mère's in residence!"

It seemed to come to Belle suddenly that she was the only person looking forward to this event with enthusiasm. Her voice trailed off. She stared at them thoughtfully, taking in their pale faces, their strange expressions.

"And just what," she asked slowly, "*have* you been doing while I've been gone?"

Chapter 11

"Very nice," Aaron whistled softly, looking around. "Very, *very* nice."

It had taken no time at all to repair the fuses. ("You see," Ginny had said, "it's perfectly simple—if you're born to it.")

"Talk about 'born to it'—" Aaron set down his cup of coffee and strolled over to squint at the signature on a pair of miniatures. "*Very* nice indeed." He straightened up and grinned at the girls.

"How about the guided tour?" he suggested. "The stately flats of England, eh?"

"Why not?" Amy grinned back. There didn't seem any harm in the idea. Provided they skimmed through the bedrooms quickly, there shouldn't be anything wrong with it. Apart from which, she and Ginny were proud of the place. The pride of possession—however temporary—almost equalling that of ownership.

She'd wronged them, though. The bedrooms brought no leers or innuendoes. Aaron and Zlot surveyed the rooms with a cool—almost professional—detachment. She wondered fleetingly if they were decorators.

Only in the master bedroom did Aaron show a sudden enthusiasm. "Nice—" He crossed the room swiftly to examine a portrait on the opposite wall. He studied it a moment then reached out and tilted the frame curiously with the back of one finger, letting it fall back into place so quickly it might never have been moved at all. "Very nice," he approved.

"The thing about these kind of flats," Zlot said with satisfaction, "you see one, you've seen them all."

"This is the only one you're likely to see." Ginny led the way back to the drawing-room. "So make the most of it. Practically everybody else in the building seems to be out of town."

"That's right," Aaron said. "This is the time of year they would be. Mustn't miss the salmon fishing and the racing and all that, you know."

They laughed, settling down and taking up their coffee cups again. Amy noticed Zlot trying to glance at his watch inconspicuously.

"Look," she said. "This has been very kind of you— helping us out like this—but don't let us keep you. I mean, I know transport closes down early here, and you both probably have to get up at some ungodly hour in the morning—"

"We don't get up mornings—" Zlot stopped as Aaron shot him a look as halting as a sudden cuff in the face.

"We work at night," Aaron said. "Late shift work. In fact, we ought to be going now. We're due on the job soon."

Amy and Ginny walked to the door with them. "Thank you again," Amy said.

"Thank *you*." Aaron bowed with a flourish and straightened up abruptly as he noticed Zlot, who had picked up the silver salver and was twisting it round in his hands searching for the hallmark.

"Mind your manners!" He snatched the salver from Zlot. "Dirtying up the nice clean silver!" While they laughed, he rubbed the smudges left by Zlot's fingers, bringing the dulled spots back to the gleaming polish of the rest of the silver.

"That's better." He restored it to the table, giving Zlot a pointed look.

"Sorry," Zlot muttered. "Apologies all round. I got carried away."

"That's better," Aaron said again. "Now let's go—or we'll be late for work."

Zlot choked off a laugh in the face of Aaron's solemn expression.

"We'll pick you up here tomorrow," Aaron told the girls. "About seven." Without waiting for their agreement, he turned and walked out. Zlot nodded and followed.

"They're funny," Ginny decided, drifting towards the window. "Aren't they funny?"

"Ummm." Amy joined her at the window, looking down on the street. They watched Aaron and Zlot emerge from the building, cross the street and turn to stare at the block of flats from the other side with a strangely alert attention.

"They don't see us," Ginny complained, waving. "What are they looking at?"

Zlot seemed to notice them then, silhouetted in the lighted window. He waved and said something to Aaron, jogging his arm.

Aaron had been staring towards the roof. He withdrew his attention immediately to beam and wave at the lighted window. He said something in return to Zlot.

Still smiling and turning frequently to wave, they moved off down the street.

"They're funny," Ginny said again. But, this time, there was an uneasy, almost questioning, note in her voice.

They were waiting in the hallway, all ready to go, when Aaron and Zlot arrived at seven. Because they were so eager not to waste one moment of an evening out in London—or because the beginnings of a faint disquiet were already stirring just below the level of consciousness?

When the doorbell rang, they stepped out briskly to meet Aaron and Zlot, closing the door with finality behind them.

"Not asking us in?" Aaron arched an eyebrow. "What's the matter—nothing needs repairing today?" Put like that, their behaviour seemed churlish. They were instantly— oddly—on the defensive.

"We don't want to waste any time—" Ginny responded so swiftly she was almost gushing. "We're on our *vacation*, after all. We don't want to waste a *moment*."

"You're in the right company, then," Aaron said. "We *never* waste our time, do we, Zlot?"

Zlot gave the curious hiccoughing gurgle that was his laugh. "Never," he agreed.

"Not even hardly ever?" Ginny was being too arch, but it seemed to be smoothing over the situation.

"You're quiet tonight," Aaron shot at Amy as they stepped into the lift. "What's the matter?"

She shrugged. She couldn't answer. She didn't really know . . .

They went to another pub. Amy and Ginny exchanged glances but, after the uneasy start to the evening, they didn't say anything. Perhaps the boys couldn't afford more expensive entertainment.

"We have to meet a bloke here," Aaron said, whether in explanation or apology was uncertain.

Zlot brought beer and cider to the rough wooden table. (They'd have to be careful, the splintery wood was death on tights.) Aaron took the seat facing the door, his back against the wall. Without seeming to, he kept constant vigil over all entrances and exits.

Again, Amy felt the stirrings of some unspecified uneasiness. She ignored it, then forgot it as Ginny and Zlot began laughing at some joke she had missed.

"Back in a mo'." Aaron rose. Amy had the vague

impression that it was in response to a figure which had appeared briefly in the doorway, signalled, and disappeared. "Keep the girls entertained." He moved swiftly to the doorway.

Zlot watched him go then moved over to take his seat. Now he was the one watching the doorway.

"Where are we, anyway?" Amy asked. She didn't like this side of the river. "Where exactly?"

"Exactly?" Zlot looked at her oddly. "That's hard to say. What do you want to know for?"

"To tell them back home," Ginny put in innocently. "Everybody's going to want to know where we've been and what we've seen."

"Oh." Zlot relaxed. "Tell them the Elephant and Castle. They'll have heard of that. That's close enough."

"But—*exactly*," Amy persisted.

"Here's Aaron." Zlot got up with relief. Over their heads he met Aaron's eyes questioningly and received an almost imperceptible nod in reply.

"Right!" Aaron beamed at them, pulling them from their seats by sheer force of the magnetic personality he suddenly switched on. "That's done, then. Let's go some place more exciting. . . ."

It wasn't the drinks—they didn't have that many. Nor was it solely—as it might have been—the rushing dizzily from one place to another, back in the bright lights of the West End. The jumping on and off of buses before they had quite stopped, the leaping into and out of taxis, ordering them to stop abruptly when they passed a place that looked enticing, the rushing into these places—and the rushing out again if they proved disappointing.

"It's all a giddy whirl," Ginny giggled. "It's a really, truly, giddy whirl."

But it wasn't. It was Aaron.

Once switched on, that forceful mesmerizing charm

had cast an enchantment over them, colouring the whole evening, dispelling all qualms. It turned them into a charmed circle of beautiful people. Everything any one of them said was brilliantly funny, every place they went into was exotic, every moment was magic. Reality slid away, becoming nothing to do with them. Rather, the only reality was their own. They seemed to be enclosed in some gossamer bubble which lent its own iridescence to the world they looked out at. Nothing could shatter it—at least not for this one evening.

Even the after-hours drinking club they wound up at seemed special rather than shoddy, exciting rather than sinister. There was no threat in the faces that turned to watch them—they were still encapsuled, safe in the protection of Aaron's magic aura. They sensed it in the way the watching eyes—hot or hostile—looked beyond them and, encountering Aaron, lost interest and looked quickly away.

All but one pair of eyes, which watched intently as Aaron herded his party across to a quiet corner. Amy was conscious of that gaze as they settled themselves and ordered.

Then the man moved, approaching them obliquely, just beyond the range of Aaron's vision. He went unnoticed until he was upon them, his hand dropping suddenly to clutch Aaron's shoulder.

Aaron jumped—and that was funny, too: the overreaction to a simple action, and the look on his face of startlement so exaggerated as to resemble fear.

Zlot seemed to be the most amused of all, as though at some private joke mysterious to the others. His hiccoughing laughter, coming in convulsing spasms as he rocked back and forth in his chair, sent Amy and Ginny off into fresh gales of laughter themselves.

Aaron didn't laugh, nor did the grim man standing over him. Neither did any of the bystanders. Rather, they seemed to shrink farther away, as though resentful of such merriment.

In other places, the onlookers had been envious or themselves amused, their sympathetic sidelong glances saying, *Enjoy yourselves, you're only young once.*

Here, there was a bitterness in the quickly-averted stares and an underlying sly satisfaction that seemed to say, *You'll find out.*

But that was funny, too. And when the man, still gripping Aaron's shoulder, said, "You owe me fifty quid," it was hilarious.

"I haven't got it," Aaron said. The colour had come back into his face and he was smiling faintly, as though it were a situation he could deal with easily.

"Don't give me that." The man shook Aaron's shoulder. "I want that money now."

"I haven't got it," Aaron repeated. "But—" he rolled his head back slowly to look upwards—"I can tell you where to get it."

"I'm listening." There was a wary note in the man's voice, but eagerness in his eyes. He wanted that money.

"Here." Aaron pulled a scrap of paper and a pencil from his pocket, scribbled rapidly, and passed the paper over his shoulder. "Go see her, chat her up a bit, make friends. She's got pots of money. Doesn't mind lending it, forgets to ask for it back. Treat her right and you can get as much as you want. More than fifty, I can tell you. I reckon that bit of paper is worth my fifty to you."

"It better be." The man took the paper and moved away. Aaron stared after him, raising his hand to massage the spot on his shoulder where he had been so tightly gripped.

But, after a momentary bewilderment, the mood of the evening descended again, too strong to be broken by any shadow of unpleasantness.

"You're cads!" Ginny giggled. "Giving away that poor

girl's name like that. Cads!" She looked across at Amy, who suddenly began to feel that it was funny too. "Do you realize we're in the company of cads?"

They all laughed then, and the bubble—which for a cold moment had constricted around them and threatened to burst—expanded and held them safe again. The clarity of sight and thought which had hovered perilously close dissolved once more into the rosy mist.

"Here's to us." Aaron raised his glass to Zlot. "The cads! Long may we rule!"

Faces turned towards them briefly again, then turned away. Ripples of hostility seemed to eddy out from the others in the room, but dissolved after lapping helplessly against the impenetrable protection of the invisible bubble. Nothing could harm them—nothing could get through to them.

"It's terribly late," Amy said guiltily, pouring them coffee in the flat. "We've made you late for work, haven't we? I'm sorry."

"That's all right," Aaron said. "No special time we have to start, is there, Zlot?"

"Come and go as we like," Zlot said. "That's how important we are in our work." His hiccoughing gurgle rose and fell, setting them all off again.

"We'll work twice as hard to catch up." Aaron's face twisted, convulsed with a silent mirth. "That's all."

"Won't be hard," Zlot choked. "Dead keen on our work, we are."

"What *do* you do?" Ginny asked curiously. "Really, what *do* you do for a living?"

"Us?" Aaron laughed aloud this time. "What would you say we do, Zlot?"

"Anyone we can," Zlot said. Their laughter rose and fell again.

"It's hopeless," Ginny complained to Amy. "They just won't be serious."

"Is this a night to be serious?" Aaron, in his turn, appealed to her. "Besides, you wouldn't believe us if we told you."

"We just did," Zlot said. Somehow, this set them all off into more fits of weak giggling. Nothing was serious—nothing was real—tonight.

Before they left, both Zlot and Aaron discreetly disappeared, separately, and at tactfully spaced intervals. They knew the way and they had been drinking quite a lot.

"We'll say good night now," Aaron said, shortly after he returned. "No, don't bother—" as they started to rise. "We'll see ourselves out. You're tired. Get your beauty sleep and we'll see you tomorrow."

"We may be a bit later than usual," Zlot put in, with unusual caution. "We've got a busy day ahead."

"But we'll be along," Aaron said firmly. "So you two just sit tight and wait for us." Already at the door, he blew them a kiss.

"We'll be seeing you."

Amy woke early in the morning. She lay, eyes closed, identifying the now-familiar sounds of London stirring around her, preparatory to the start of another day: the rumble of the double-decker buses, becoming more frequent as service picked up to meet the approaching rush hour; the strange, almost sinister, whine of an electric milk float trundling down the street with the morning deliveries; the melodious lilt of the Westminster chimes from the oversized Victorian clock in the front hall sounding the half-hour. Perhaps London didn't have its street cries any more, but you could never lie awake of a morning and mistake it for New York or Chicago. You knew you were in London.

There was something else in the atmosphere this morning, though. She grew aware of it gradually, as she awakened more fully. A curious sense of oppression was there, waiting to engulf her when she moved, ready to wrap itself around her when she threw back the covers and stood up.

There was no reason for it. She had never been one for gloom or dark depressions. And she was on vacation—having a wonderful time. So why was she lying here, practically cowering at the thought of getting out of bed and facing the morning?

It was ridiculous. She got up quickly, before she could think of any more idiocies and put on her robe. Even then, it was a bit chilly. That was probably what was wrong with her—her blood sugar level was too low. After breakfast, she'd feel fine again.

Also, she drew back the curtains with a faint sigh, it was raining. Not just the misty rain they had grown accustomed to—rather liked—here, but a relentless torrential downpour. The sort of rain associated with hurricane weather back home—the tail-end of some tropical havoc still lashing out to destroy as it worked its way inland and up the Atlantic coast from its devastated place of birth.

She put the kettle on the gas and listened for a moment. No sounds of stirring from Ginny's room. Ginny was usually a sound sleeper, especially in weather like this. For that matter, she usually slept more deeply herself when it rained—something to do with barometric pressure, people claimed. It could also be responsible for this sense of impending doom which had not been dispelled, just lightened slightly, by the acts of getting up and starting breakfast.

When Ginny got up and there was someone to talk to, she would undoubtedly feel better. Perhaps she ought to wake Ginny. When the kettle boiled, she could do so—making a joke of it—by bringing her a cup of tea, in the time-honoured English tradition. Even if Ginny didn't get up, they could have the tea and gossip for a while,

planning the day. It would be a good day for shopping.
They still had their lists of relatives and friends who would
require or expect presents and souvenirs. Today would be
a good day for working their way through the stores,
reducing the lists as much as possible.

There was a rustle and snap from the front hall door
as something was thrust through the letter flap. Mail from
home, perhaps. Possibly even a card from Belle to let
them know when she was returning. The thought brightened her morning mood a bit and Amy started for the
front door to see what had fallen on to the mat.

She paused in the drawing-room to pull back the
curtains and open the windows. The damp fresh air was
mildly invigorating and she leaned out, breathing deeply,
before moving back into the room to continue on her way
to pick up the post.

The sense of something wrong—not just mood or
imagination, but something physically wrong—halted her
on the threshhold and pulled her back into the room. She
turned slowly, at first not registering what she saw. Or,
rather, what she didn't see.

"GINNY!" She called, her voice a croak of despera-
tion. "GINNY!" Still she hadn't seen it, only the choking
grip of that now-pounced terror and despondency which
had been awaiting her since she woke told her that it had
happened.

Not moving from the doorway, she let her gaze travel
across and around the room. It stopped, hovering, on the
small dark circles of unfaded wallpaper where the miniatures had hung.

Now suddenly—rudely—educated, she knew where
else to look. Where the small, light, portable, easily-
disposed-of valuables had been. The enamel snuff boxes
from the side-table—gone. The empty mantel—no Chelsea figures there.

"What's the matter?" Ginny was behind her, drawn

so swiftly by the urgency of her call that she hadn't bothered to stop to put on robe or slippers. She stood there shivering, toes curling. "You look as though you've seen a ghost. It can't be that bad."

For answer, Amy pointed. Ginny blinked, trying to focus, to bring eyes and mind out of their early morning haze and take in what had happened.

Silently, insistently, Amy kept pointing, swinging her finger to the wall, the mantel, the side-table, and then starting again. Desperately and without hope, she prayed that Ginny might know something—have some reasonable explanation.

"Oh, my God!" Ginny groaned. It had registered at last. They stared at each other in consternation.

"Look," Ginny said, "it must be some mistake—or a joke. That's it. It *has* to be a joke." Neither of them smiled.

"I heard the postman," Amy said. "I was on my way to get the mail and—"

"The mail—" Ginny said. "That's it! I'll bet they've sent a note. Just to say 'Ha-ha' or something—" She turned and hurried for the front door.

Amy followed more slowly. She watched Ginny, as though through the wrong end of a telescope, as Ginny stooped to pick up the familiar blue envelopes from the mat. Three of them. There had been nothing local at all, she had not expected that there would be.

Unlike Ginny, who was still frantically shuffling them, as though the right legerdemain would produce a white envelope containing a merry note to put everything right again.

"Perhaps the next post—" Ginny was not willing to give up. "It's too early—" She broke off; following Amy's gaze to the console-table.

The empty console-table.

They met each other's eyes again, remembering Zlot,

clowning with the silver salver. Checking for the hallmark to make sure it was solid silver.

"Well—" Ginny's slow soft voice was a whisper of defeat—"I guess we'd better believe it . . ."

Chapter 12

They were putting the lights on down in the mews. First in the kitchens at the rear of the tiny houses, the light ghosting through halls and front rooms with fire-fly evanescence as housewives and au pairs worked on the impending meals, doors swinging open and shut behind them as they moved about. Later, the lights would be switched on in the front rooms to provide a welcoming warmth for returning spouses to home in on.

Then the streetlamps sprang into a quiet glow—not quite gas lamps, there weren't many of those left, but constructed in the old style, perhaps some of the earliest electric streetlamps. They blended in with the atmosphere of the mews, their discreet radiance lightening the area without becoming obtrusive. She almost liked this quiet hour—as much as she could like anything—even though it meant the night was almost here. But night brought no fear now, she wasn't a child. She wasn't anything any more, except a watcher—and a waiter.

The house of the Yellow Lady was always the last to come alight. It must be because of some personal idiosyncrasy—and not from any desire to pinch pennies, too many lights came on for that, and stayed on too long. The Yellow Lady was obviously an insomniac. One moment— the last possible moment before the complete inky blackness of night—the house was dark, the next moment it was aglow from top to bottom, and it was larger than the smaller houses along the side of the mews. It seemed to shed light like a stage setting, and it was somehow comforting to think of the golden indomitable old lady moving through the golden radiance far into the night.

Across the room, the door opened. Amy turned sharply—she had heard no step outside.

"I'm going off duty in a few minutes." Nurse Jellicoe slid into the room. "I came to see if there was anything you wanted before I left—"

"No," Amy said sharply, turning back to the window.

"And to sneak a cigarette," Nurse Jellicoe persisted, her face a little pinker, and wrestling the packet of cigarettes from her pocket.

Amy glanced at her in time to catch the faint flicker of distaste that crossed her face as she lit the final cigarette of the day. Poor little Nurse Jellicoe—how pleased she would be when this assignment ended and she could go back to being a non-smoker again.

"It's been a beautiful day for this time of year." They ought to give little Policewoman/Nurse Jellicoe a bonus— she never gave up. "Quite like summer. What is it you people call it?"

"Indian Summer," Amy responded automatically, without thinking.

"That's it!" Nurse Jellicoe moved forward, beaming. Encouraged, Amy saw, by the sort of sudden response they had all almost stopped hoping for.

Pointedly, silently, she turned her face back to the window, upset by the thought that her guard had been lowered, even momentarily. She had been so careful, kept them all at arm's length for so long that she had believed it had become a habit, that she no longer had to watch her responses. Ordinarily, she hadn't. But something was different tonight, something was out of the ordinary. Something noticed only by her subconscious as yet, which was sending signals interrupting her usual patterns to try to jolt her into awareness. But what? Was it that Aaron was nearby? This strange disruption a result of his thought waves seeking her out—?

"Sitting here in the dark!" Nurse Jellicoe had retreated as far as the light switch and now flooded brightness into the room from the overhead light. "People will think we're out of our minds!"

And that was what was wrong.

"The lights haven't come on," Amy said. "Her house is still dark."

"But I've just put them on—" Nurse Jellicoe broke off, obviously realizing that she had started out at a crosspurpose. She moved swiftly to the window, coming up behind Amy silently.

"You're right," she said. "Her house *is* still dark."

They remained together at the window, unexpectedly united for a moment in their sudden concern. So little Nurse Jellicoe, too, had spent enough time at windows looking down on the life in the mews to be able to identify the patterns and customs of that life. Amy wondered how many bored hours Nurse Jellicoe had employed in that way, keeping guard, waiting for meal times, changes of shift, or any other activities that might give her an excuse to enter the room again on one of her endless attempts to make contact, gain confidence.

"Come away from the window," Nurse Jellicoe said urgently, pulling the chair back.

She made a perfect target there, Amy realized, with the brilliantly lit room behind her. But how silly of Nurse Jellicoe to imagine that she cared. Of course, it must be her own job she was worrying about. It could do her little good professionally to lose a case—or a patient—whichever

her profession might be. And she was the one who had
put the light on, to silhouette anyone at the window. Too
bad. Let her worry.

As the chair continued its backward progress, Amy
stepped out of it, returning to stand beside the window,
looking down on the mews.

"Oh! Have it your way, then!" There was a clatter as
Nurse Jellicoe relinquished the empty chair and rushed
for the light switch. The room pitched into blackness, then
a dim glow sprang up as she switched on the bedside
reading-lamp.

"That's better." Nurse Jellicoe came back to the window. The light illumined the room, but was too faint to
provide guidance for a marksman.

Not now.

The floodlights on the roof of the nursing home had
been switched on. No one could fire into that blinding
glare of light. That was why they were there.

Or, one of the reasons. Perhaps the authorities, too,
knew that Aaron would come across the rooftops. ("They
don't change their methods much," a policeman had said.
"Set in their ways, like.") Aaron's way was the way of the
cat burglar.

There had never been lights on the roof before she
came. The reactions of the people in the mews had told
her that. Even now, curtains were being hurriedly closed
in upstairs nursery windows, so that the bright lights
would not wake the infants. Some mothers cast harassed
impatient glances at the roof before disappearing from
view behind the curtains. Others—one or two—lingered,
as though aware that something was different. They turned
vaguely questioning heads to look up and down the mews,
perhaps not even aware of what they were seeking: the
strange absence of light from the house at the end of the
mews. Then these, too, closed their curtains, but with a
lingering reluctance, as though dissatisfied at not being

able to trace the source of their uneasiness. But they had no time to waste pondering, their own busy lives waited, behind them in the cradle, downstairs in the kitchen and in the front door that would open soon. Their last sense of unexplained disquiet would disappear as soon as they turned away from the windows.

"There!" Nurse Jellicoe said, on a small sigh of relief.

While Amy had been watching the curtains close in the cottages across the street, a light had come on in the Yellow Lady's house. Just one light and not a very bright one, but it was better than nothing. Perhaps the others would come on now. She watched, curiously intent, as though it had something to do with her. As though she had a right to care about the welfare of a stranger she had never met and never would meet.

"It's all right now," Nurse Jellicoe said. "Come away from the window."

But, when Amy turned, she saw that the expression on Nurse Jellicoe's face did not match the confidence in her voice. She was frowning slightly and there was a new, unidentifiable look in the eyes which were still trained on the house at the end of the mews.

"Come along." She cleared her face of all expression as she noticed Amy watching her. She was brisk and brusque again, the mask back in place.

"No," Amy said. "I want to stay here."

"Oh—" Nurse Jellicoe seemed to debate the point silently, then shrugged. "Stay then," she said. "I can't. I'll have to leave now. I—I have a date."

"Have fun," Amy said tonelessly. She deliberately let her mind go blank. It was a world she had withdrawn from, would never see again. Dates were for other girls, like Nurse Jellicoe, with a lifetime ahead of them. She herself had only one more date pending. With Aaron. When he kept it—

"Good night." Nurse Jellicoe was already at the door, drawn by the promise of life and laughter outside. In the morning. she would have to report back here for duty again, but tonight she would be with friends, off-duty and free to be herself. It was not surprising that she could hardly wait.

"Good night." Despite her eagerness to get away, she had waited until Amy replied, perhaps feeling that she was at last making some headway in forging a link between them.

Now the door closed behind her and Amy turned back to the window.

As always, the character of the mews changed with the grotesque distortion of the familiar shadows caused by the floodlights on the roof. It became a bearpit, with monster shapes swelling and dwindling as the rising wind began to sway trees and bushes. It was the time when Amy usually moved away from the window, drawing the curtains as the other people in the mews did, but without gaining any of their sense of security from the action.

Tonight she remained, looking down. The shadows were darker and deeper without the glow from the Yellow Lady's house. Strange how the subdued lighting reflected into the mews from the radiance within the house could make that much difference. But why hadn't all the lights gone on tonight?

She pressed her forehead against the window, straining to see into the rooms of the house. The curtains were not drawn—had never been drawn—against the invading light from the roof of the nursing home. The brightness within had acted as its own backfire to counteract the glare. It had also, she realized now, softened the night harshness of the mews.

Was that another light being lit on the ground floor? She craned her neck, wondering if she might open the

window and lean out. Immediately, something in her mind
vetoed that idea. Why make it too easy for Aaron?

It *was* a light, though, towards the back of the house
and, even as she watched, the thin dark silhouette of the
au pair appeared at the front windows in the unprece-
dented task of drawing the curtains.

Was the Yellow Lady ill? Had the au pair called the
doctor and taken it upon herself to draw the curtains
against any possibly prying eyes in the mews?

Which would mean her. Amy drew back flushing.
Perhaps nothing was wrong. More probably, they had
discovered they were constantly overlooked, perhaps caught
her watching, and were reacting with the classic gesture
signalling, *Mind your own business.*

But her business was finished—or almost. It came as
a shock that she could have forgotten that, even for so
short a space of time as it took to spare a moment of
concern for someone else.

About to draw the curtain herself, she stopped. A
slant of light knifed into the mews from an open door. She
leaned forward again.

The front door of the house at the end of the mews
had opened. Again the tall thin silhouette of the au pair
appeared, like a black tongue of flame in the sudden blaze
of light in the doorway. She stepped just outside, drawing
the door shut behind her. In the reflection of the overhead
glare, she could be clearly discerned, turning her head
slowly to survey the mews, pausing, eyes probing, at
every shadow to make certain it was just what it appeared.

Now what? Invisible hackles rose at the nape of Amy's
neck. It was not the first time she had had this reaction to
the sight of the au pair. Why should an incompetent
untrustworthy au pair affect her so? It was the Yellow
Lady's problem. If she couldn't manage her servants, why
should an unknown stranger, looking on from above, worry
about it?

The au pair, obviously satisfied, nodded to herself and slipped back inside the house, not quite closing the door behind her. The narrow sliver of light kept Amy as immovably glued to the window as the rustle and thump of a scene being changed behind a closed curtain kept a theatregoer taut in his seat.

Then the door opened again. Just wide enough for another figure to slip out. Head bowed, blonde mink coat clutched tightly around her, the Yellow Lady emerged slowly. The au pair followed, to stand in the doorway, door again pulled partially closed behind her, to watch the Yellow Lady's progress down the mews with an anxiety that had never been apparent in her bearing before.

Yet, Amy pressed closer to the window, the au pair was right to worry—she had never seen the Yellow Lady look like this before.

Her head was bent, chin buried in the collar of her coat, her shoulders hunched as though against a cold too great to bear—or some unimaginable blow of fate. That must be the answer. That was why people drew curtains and sat in darkened houses. Some bad news—the death of a loved one—had bowed that dauntless lady to the grief that encompasses everyone at some time or other. Was she on her way to a deathbed? Or to select personally the flowers that would be a final tribute to some dear one whose loss must be overwhelming in its finality?

The unsteady progress down the mews continued erratically, as though the Yellow Lady might be blinded by secret tears behind the protective veil she had chosen to place between herself and the world.

With a shrug of dismissal, the au pair turned and re-entered the house, shutting the door firmly behind her, as though disclaiming responsibility for the English madwoman who insisted on going out when she was so obviously unfit to do so. Without that sliver of additional light, the mews grew darker.

Then, in the increased darkness, the Yellow Lady missed her footing, stumbled into one of the black pools of shadows, and nearly fell. Hands flung out, coat flying loosely, she balanced herself just in time, dropping her handbag as she did so.

For a long moment, she stood there, wobbling slightly on heels that did not allow for unsteadiness, and looked down at the handbag at her feet as though it were a million miles away. Then, very cautiously—as though new, or heretofore unacknowledged, pains in her back were making themselves felt—she stooped and slowly retrieved the handbag. She tucked it back under her arm, draped the coat more tightly around her and continued—with renewed caution—towards the exit of the mews. This time she seemed to be actively seeking the shelter of the shadows, as though they were her allies now, shielding her from eyes that might note her weakness.

Amy stepped back sharply and snatched the curtains shut. Not even to herself—to herself, least of all—did she want to admit the pang she felt at seeing the heretofore indomitable old lady brought low. What was it to her? Nothing. *Nothing!*

Awkwardly, she pulled the chair and the needlework frame over beside the bed and settled so that the light from the bedside table fell upon the needlework. Trying to make her mind a blank, she carefully measured a length of silk.

The picture was so close to finished, perhaps tonight she would finish it. Was it worth starting another? Had she time?

Strange, the way they had spoken about Aaron—they had seemed to feel he was essentially harmless because of his work. At best a confidence man, at worst a cat burglar—"no real harm in them," they said. They didn't know Aaron as she did.

And why were cat burglars supposed to be harmless? Was it because of that deceptively domestic word 'cat' in their title? Was a cat gentle and harmless?

Ask the mouse.

Chapter 13

Belle listened quietly as they tried to explain. At only one point did she make any move. When they told of Aaron inspecting the painting in the bedroom, she stood abruptly and went into the master bedroom. She crossed and lifted the painting from the wall, rather than tilting it with a furtive finger as he had done.

By this time, they were not surprised to see the wall safe behind the painting. They knew now that Aaron did not waste his interest on anything unprofitable.

"It hasn't been touched, thank heaven," Belle said, replacing the painting. "But he's right about one thing, though. All these flats *are* alike. And the wall-safe-behind-the-painting idea was the latest thing when they were built. Super secret. Now, of course—" she shrugged— "everyone knows. First place they look. It's a wonder we continue to use them, except, of course, that they're convenient and somehow one never expects—"

Belle broke off and went over to the window. "So many flats, so many tenants," she murmured. "And so many of them out of town. It could be weeks before some of them return."

"The whole building could be cleared out by then." Ginny voiced the thought in both their minds.

"I think not," Belle said decisively. "The first thing—"

she led them back to the drawing-room, collecting a pad and pencil on her way—"is to find out precisely what is missing here. We'll start with the things you noticed missing, then we'll check everything else against the insurance inventory. After that, we'll have a clearer idea of how we stand and we can start things moving."

They followed abjectly. This was a new Belle, so competent, cool and collected. Knowing what to do, completely in command. She was the same age as themselves, yet they suddenly felt like schoolchildren beside her.

Mercifully, she did not treat them as schoolchildren. In a way, it would have been easier to bear if she had. They felt, obscurely, that they deserved some kind of punishment—at the least, a scolding.

"I'm sorry," Amy said. "I'm so terribly sorry—"

"Don't—" Belle cut her off. "It's over and done. We can't change anything by agonizing. All we can do is go on from here." Belle smiled, and it came to Amy that she was actually enjoying the challenge this situation had brought.

"But won't you get in the most awful trouble?" Ginny asked. "What will your family say? All their lovely treasures gone."

"Not quite all." Belle smiled more broadly, looking around the room. It was true. If they hadn't known for a fact which pieces were missing, their absence might not have been noticed by a casual eye. The room was still amply adorned.

"It's just as well, though—" Belle's smile faded—"that they didn't get into the safe. I'll check that later, but I believe Gran'mère left a few family pieces in it. She usually does, in case she wants to come down to town for dinner and the theatre. Then she needn't worry about carrying jewellery with her. If they'd made off with the diamonds, it might have got a bit hairy."

"They couldn't have opened the safe without us knowing," Amy said. "They weren't out of the room long enough.

And," she added honestly, "they probably thought they had enough time to do it later. They might have thought we wouldn't even notice anything was missing. We're guests here, after all, and wouldn't be expected to be familiar with every little treasure. They already knew—" her voice tightened with the beginnings of self-loathing— "that neither of us was very observant."

"Let it be!" Belle said sharply. "You can't keep blaming yourself. Something like this might have happened to anyone at any time."

"But it happened to *us*," Ginny said, the awareness of such an encroachment of the unthinkable into their hitherto sheltered lives making a wavering shock wave pattern of her usually placid tones. "And they even told us so. They admitted it straight out and laughed about it. They were laughing at *us*—because we were too stupid to believe them."

"Well, we believe them now," Amy said grimly.

"And they're coming back tonight," Ginny said. "I'll just bet they think they're going to pick up a lot more stuff before we realize it. They think they can plunder this flat right under our noses."

"Then they're going to learn differently," Amy said. Momentarily, they had both forgotten Belle, she stood to one side, watching them. "They're not taking anything else—we'll make them give back what they stole last night."

"How?" Belle asked. The practicality of the question stopped them both, bringing them out of the euphoria of righteous indignation. They looked at each other uncertainly, then looked to Belle.

"And what of the others?" she asked. "From what you've told me, they never intended to confine their attentions solely to this flat. They've perhaps used it as much as a master floor plan for the building as for anything else."

"They—said they were going to work last night," Ginny recalled uneasily. "You mean, you think—?"

"I think," Belle said firmly, "it's time we got some professional advice about this."

Belle retreated into the master bedroom to make her telephone calls. While admitting her right to do this, it did not make them feel any better.

"She's probably checking the safe while she's in there," Ginny said gloomily. "Opening it, I mean, and counting the diamonds—or what have you."

"Well, face it," Amy said, finding slight release in a brutality directed more against herself than against Ginny, "would *you* invite *us* to watch you dial the combination if the positions were reversed?"

"God—how I wish they had been!" Ginny dropped on to the sofa and covered her face with her hands. "How did we get *into* this mess?"

"How do we get out of it? That's more to the point."

They heard the telephone dial spin in the bedroom. Belle would be dialling the insurance company first, she had told them. And, after that—"Someone . . ." she had said lightly. The Belles of this world always knew the right Someones to contact. Especially over here in this older, stranger, world. Perhaps that was the secret of their survival in a society which had periodically made almost a ritual of declaring their sort outmoded, outdated, and a historically impossible survivor—like the duck-billed platypus. Like the duck-billed platypus, however, they continued to breed and thrive, serenely conscious that their obituaries were premature.

"Ginny—you can't!" Amy protested, as Ginny moved up to the bedroom door and listened.

Making a face, Ginny motioned for silence. Amy had to comply. Otherwise, Belle might hear a disagreement, come to the door and discover Ginny. Unthinkable—especially in the light of the betrayal of hospitality they had already been guilty of. With a faint moan, Amy slumped into a chair.

"No, you're right." Ginny left the door and came back to the sofa again. "I can't. And besides—" the ghost of her old mischievous smile haunted the corners of her mouth briefly and disappeared—"I can't hear a thing, anyway." She put her hands to her forehead again. "Oh, God, I just want to die!"

"I want to die, too," Amy agreed.

"Well, I don't want to die!" Belle re-entered the room, eyes sparkling. "Buck up, you two. It's not the end of the world."

"Prove it," Ginny said.

"For one thing, we're covered by insurance," Belle enumerated briskly. "For another, the insurers think there's a good chance of getting the miniatures, and possibly the Chelsea figures, back. It seems there are all sorts of 'hot lines' between the police and antique dealers' associations, and descriptions of stolen goods—especially such easily identifiable pieces—are circulated to dealers almost within hours. So, if they've already bought the stolen goods, they surrender them to the police. Or, if the thief comes in and tries to sell them the articles, they can call the police. Either way, the odds are awfully good that we'll recover the property."

"That will be a help," Ginny said, sounding a bit more cheerful. She stole a sideways look at Amy. "But—"

"But, at the fastest," Amy said, "nothing much could be circulated and read before tomorrow and—and they're coming back here tonight. We'll see them before anyone else does."

"Oh no, we won't," Belle said. "At least, not the way *you* mean. I've also been talking to a friend of Gran'mère's at the Home Office. We're going there now. We'll have tea with him and some people he thinks we ought to meet. You can make a statement, and give them a description, and the police will be able to move into action. When your . . . friends . . . arrive, the police will intercept them downstairs and arrest them. You needn't ever speak to them or see them again. At least, not until they're in the dock—where they belong."

"Really?" It sounded too good to be true, too smooth, too simple, but they wanted to believe it. And Belle had said so, this new Belle who had shown an unsuspected ability to meet a crisis and surmount it.

"I promise you," Belle said firmly. "Now put on your things and we'll get a taxi to the Home Office. Next week, we'll take that trip to Paris—you can't go home without having seen Paris—and we'll have a lovely time. In another few weeks, we'll hardly remember what all this fuss was about."

"I suppose so," Amy said dubiously.

"I promise you," Belle repeated, secure in her command of the situation. "Some day we'll laugh about it all."

Chapter 14

The formalities had not taken long. Flowing smoothly on a tide of tea, inquiries as to the health of Belle's various relatives, reminiscences and snippets of advice, they had scarcely seemed like formalities at all.

It had been strongly recommended to them that they did not return to the flat that evening; or, having returned, that they did not venture out again until morning. Talking it over among themselves, they had voted for the latter. They had reached a stage of emotional exhaustion where any further activity was unthinkable. They intended to lock themselves in, have an early night—if necessary, with the aid of the sleeping tablets it seemed Sybilla always left in the bathroom medicine cabinet—and hope that the world would look brighter and more hopeful in the morning.

"Right," Belle said, and returned to the inner office. She remained in there for perhaps longer than would have been necessary to report their decision, but they didn't bother to remark on it. If she had thought of something else she wished to discuss, it was no business of theirs. They had done enough—and it was not for them to remark on the length of time it might take to straighten out the trouble they had caused. Chastened as schoolchildren waiting outside the headmaster's office, they awaited Belle's return with the patience born of despair. She might for-give them, but it would be a long time before they forgave themselves.

When they got back to the block of flats, there was a policeman casually patrolling on the other side of the street and a determined-looking man in plain clothes read-ing a newspaper in the lobby. Belle nodded graciously to both of them as they went past. Looking back over their shoulders, Amy and Ginny saw the unobtrusive move-ment of hand to mouth which meant a message was being conveyed into a small walkie-talkie. They were being checked in.

They stood well back in the lift. Preoccupied, Belle had not bothered to close the inner door. They watched the floor levels slide past relentlessly. Amy found that she was already wondering how soon they could go home, whether it would be possible to cut short their planned visit, or whether that might make everything seem worse. There would be too many explanations needed at home, and Belle would certainly dispute their changing their plans. Belle, she suspected with a twinge of resentment, was enjoying all this.

"Here we are." The lift snicked to a stop at the fourth floor and Belle pulled back the outer door. "You'll want something light, I think." Belle herded them down the corridor. "I'll make soup and sandwiches. Will that be all right?"

"Fine," they chorused dispiritedly. At that moment, it seemed immaterial whether they ever ate again.

"It will be quick and easy." Belle used her key, letting them into the flat. "And nourishing. You'll feel better after some food. When was the last time you ate?"

They shook their heads. Food had been outside their consideration for so long it was hard to remember.

"Yesterday, I guess," Ginny said. "We had a kind of a meal with—"

"Yesterday!" Belle cut in with tactful horror. "No wonder you're coming apart at the seams. I'll get food started right away. You two put your things away and come out to the kitchen—we'll eat there." . . . Amazingly, they felt better after eating, although they had been sure that nothing could ever help. Belle had been right about that, perhaps she would turn out to be right about other things, too.

"Maybe it *will* all seem like a dream after we get back from Paris," Ginny said hopefully.

"A nightmare," Amy said, without discounting the implication behind Ginny's statement. Given enough time, a coating of distance, perspective and other diversions might blur the painful reality. Given enough time.

They could hear Belle humming in the kitchen as she tidied up the dishes and waited for the percolator to begin perking. She had chased them into the drawing-room and would bring in the coffee when it was ready.

"Belle's been so marvellous about this," Ginny said. "When I think what *some* people would have—"

"Don't!" Amy shuddered. "And we'd deserve it—that's the worst of it. I think I'd almost feel better if she'd shout at us a bit."

"I know what you mean," Ginny said. "It doesn't seem possible—" She broke off, hearing Belle's footsteps coming down the hall.

"Here we are." Belle brought in the tray and set it on the coffee-table. "White for everybody, isn't it?" She began to pour, still humming absently, " 'Once in love with Amy' . . ."

"Belle!" Amy stiffened. "Belle—don't!"

"Don't what?" Belle looked up, startled. "Amy, what's the matter? You're white as a sheet."

"That song—" Amy said. She hadn't mentioned it to

anyone, not even Ginny. It had seemed a private joke at the time, and she hadn't thought of it since.

"Song?" Belle cocked her head to one side, as though listening, then hummed a bit more. " . . . 'Tear up your list, it's Amy . . .' Yes, that *is* an old one, isn't it? But—"

"You've never sung it before," Amy said.

"No, I don't suppose I have," Belle agreed. "I don't know what put it into my head just now." She paused, thinking. "Oh, yes, I do. Someone was whistling it just outside the kitchen door. Someone going down the back stairs. I suppose I simply picked up the tune, the way one does."

"Outside the kitchen door," Amy said faintly. She looked above and beyond Belle, waiting now. She hadn't long to wait.

"Yes, what's—?" Belle turned, following her gaze.

He stood in the doorway, seeming to fill it, and surveyed the room carefully. Finding no one else there, he stepped inside warily, alert as some wild animal to a trap that might be lurking. Zlot followed him.

"Hello, Amy," Aaron said.

"How did you get in here?" Belle leaped to her feet, facing Aaron indignantly.

"It wasn't all that hard." He glanced down at her with amusement. "You must be Belle. The girls are losing their manners, it looks as if no one's going to introduce me. I'm Aaron, and that's Zlot."

"Please leave at once." Belle ignored the hand he held out.

"Now, that isn't friendly," he said. "Zlot and I thought we'd join you for coffee." He motioned with a silver-tipped ebony walking-stick he was carrying. "Zlot!"

Zlot moved forward and placed two more cups and saucers on the coffee-table. He must have collected them on his way through the kitchen. He nodded to Amy and Ginny, his beard twitching with amusement.

"Where did you get that walking-stick?" Belle demanded sharply. "That belongs to Mr. Price upstairs."

"My compliments to him on his good taste," Aaron said. "I like it. I think it suits me, don't you?" He waved the ebony stick towards Amy questioningly.

"You haven't harmed Mr. Price?" Belle looked ceiling-wards anxiously. "He's all right?"

"He's not even there," Aaron said. "Must be a nice old bloke—sent a postcard to his char—'Having a lovely time in Estoril. Will be away an extra fortnight.' "

"Oooh." Belle subsided into a chair thankfully.

"That's better," Aaron said, accepting the cup of coffee Zlot handed him and sitting on the sofa beside Amy. "What makes you think we'd harm anyone? We don't work that way. It's all nice and civilized. Knock on the door, if anyone opens it, mutter something, go in, bang on a couple of pipes, thank them and leave again. That's all there is to it. If nobody answers the door, we open it ourselves—"

Amy edged away from him until stopped by the arm of the sofa. She sipped at her coffee. It was too hot—she was too hot. She swept her arm under her hair, letting the air cool the back of her neck but, when she took her arm away, the hair fell back into place, enclosing her claustrophobically, making her hotter than before. The place, the people, seemed to recede until she might have been looking at them through the wrong end of a telescope. There was only the heat and the sense of slowly stifling.

She swept her arm under her hair again, this time leaning against the back of the sofa so that, when she dropped her arm, her hair remained draped over the back of the sofa. That was a faint improvement. She cradled the coffee-cup in her hands. Strange that her hands should be so icy cold when the rest of her seemed to be in an oven.

Except for her feet, which also felt ice-encrusted and at some great distance from her. She tightened her grip on her cup. Suddenly, the worst imaginable disaster seemed that she might drop the cup and stain the carpet with her coffee.

"What I don't understand," Belle said coldly, "is how you got into the building at all. The police were going to intercept you. They must have had a guard on the back door—they couldn't have overlooked it."

"Interesting you should say that." Aaron gazed across at her thoughtfully. "We noticed the police ourselves—but that was when we were trying to get out."

"We never *left* the building!" Zlot, squatting on the floor, gave his hiccoughing gurgle. "Worked all night, we did. One flat after another. Kipped down for a while in one of them, then back to work again."

"We left once," Aaron corrected, "about three o'clock this morning. Brought out a nice bit of stuff and put it away for safekeeping. We came back about half past four, worked some more, then took a few hours' rest. Back to work again, and another neat little load ready to take away, when we found the coppers blocking our exit. So we had a little talk and we said to each other, 'Do you suppose the girl-friends could have had anything to do with this?' And we decided to come and see. We didn't realize your chum—" he waved the ebony stick towards Belle—"had come back and decided to deal herself in on the game."

"How do you know she had anything to do with it?" Ginny's shoe had fallen off and her toes were curling in anguish, marring the dignified effect she was aiming for. "How do you know we didn't send for the police ourselves?"

"Now you wouldn't do a thing like that," Aaron said. "Why should you? I thought we understood each other."

"You can't mean—" Amy began, but broke off. Probably he had. "Do you actually mean," she asked wonderingly, "that you thought we'd set up our friends for you to steal from?"

"Why not?" His eyes were cold hard agates. "Better women than you have done it for me."

"You shouldn't have got the police in," Zlot said sorrowfully. "That wasn't very nice. Now you'll have to get rid of them again. You'll have to go and see them and confess you've been silly girls and you found the stuff you thought you'd lost. The char just put it away when she was cleaning, or something."

"That's right," Aaron said. "You're going to sound a bit stupid, I'm afraid, but the police are used to that. Mixed-up witnesses, who don't know what they're talking about. It's all in a day's work."

"You can't get away with *that!*" Belle said, her very triumph showing how close she thought the idea came to being workable. "The police aren't here just on my account. They know the whole story. They've contacted the caretaker and they're checking on all the unoccupied flats. A couple of flat owners have been contacted and they're coming back to town to take a look—they'll be able to tell what's missing. By this time, the police will know what's been going on."

"Now that," Aaron said softly, "is too bad. That's just too bad. You shouldn't have done that."

Belle laughed aloud then, actually laughed. A peal of genuine laughter, in which triumph mingled with contempt. When she stopped laughing, her face retained certain of the lines, combined with a curious coldness around the eyes and mouth. She looked strangely unreal—older, but superb.

It was a foreshadowing of the future, Amy decided, still watching through the reversed telescope. Belle would look like this permanently in another twenty-five or thirty years. She would face diplomatic receptions, rebellious servants, friends and enemies, perhaps even riots and mutinies in some distant corner of the globe with the same cold, slightly amused aplomb. She would be just as certain of her ability to handle the situation, just as certain that she was in the right. And, presumably, there would be others who were grateful that she was there to take over and rescue them from the difficulties that they had got themselves into. The world would always need its Belles and be thankful for them.

"No." Aaron was still shaking his head. "That wasn't wise at all. Now we'll have to do it the hard way. You'll have to come with us when we leave and take us past your friends on the doors."

"No, we won't," Belle declared. "And you wouldn't find it easy to try to force us to. We'd fight. And there are three of us to two of you. You're outnumbered."

"Yes," Aaron said, with dangerous quietness. "I've been thinking about that."

Somehow, it had come down to a personal duel between Aaron and Belle. Only the occasional venomous side glance he shot at Amy showed that he was still aware of her existence, that, in some tortuous passage deep in his twisted mind, he was beginning to blame her for his predicament.

Zlot crouched on the floor, head turning from Aaron to Belle, like a spectator at a tennis match. He was relaxed but alert, confident that Aaron would win in the end. Now and then he grinned at Ginny, seeming faintly hurt to receive no answering gleam of humour from her. He acted as though this were all some kind of game. Perhaps, for him, it was.

Aaron knew better, the knowledge flickered in his eyes. He could see the bars closing in on him—and he'd never be able to live behind bars. For him, it was a matter of life and death.

And so, suddenly, it became a matter of life and death for all of them.

Eyes narrowed, Aaron surveyed them carefully, like a gambler assessing his hand to choose the best card to discard. Some unspoken signal passed between him and Zlot, and Zlot stood up abruptly, poised on the balls of his feet, ready for whatever action might come next.

"I think," Aaron said slowly, "we need a diversion. Something to pull the coppers away from the front entrance." His gaze travelled thoughtfully to the window.

The doorbell rang. Only Belle remained unstartled by this sudden intrusion from the outside world. Amy realized that she had been expecting it.

"It's too late! They're at the door." Belle started triumphantly to open the door. Zlot made a move as though to stop her, but Aaron shook his head.

"They said they'd look in to make sure we were all right," Belle flung back over her shoulder. "You've had it. You can't divert your way out of *this*—you'll have to surrender!"

Aaron shrugged, his arm stretched out along the back of the sofa. "In that case, we might as well make ourselves comfortable." His dark eyes rested mordantly on Amy. "Have a cigarette."

"I don't want a cigarette," she said.

"No?" The answer seemed to amuse him. "When *I* smoke," he said, "*everybody* smokes!"

There was the brief pungent odor of lighter fluid, the leap of a spark.

"Amy!" Ginny rose, screaming. "Your hair!" Zlot moved forward, grabbing Ginny, pinioning her arms, holding her in front of him like a shield.

Amy leaped to her feet, felt the push from behind that sent her stumbling towards the hallway, was aware of the crackle of flashes she could not escape because she carried them with her. Screaming, she began to run, her hands flailing at her hair. The blazing tendrils curled round her hands, imprisoning them in a mesh of flame.

Belle had just opened the door. Amy ran through it, screaming. Startled, the two men at the door stepped back momentarily.

"Christ!" one of them said. They ran after her, catching her as she fled, spinning her to the floor and beating at the flames with their hands. One of them ripped his coat off and tried to wrap it around her head to smother the flashes. Before the folds of material fell over her eyes, she saw what was happening at the other end of the hallway.

Zlot, pushing Ginny before him, started down the stairs. Aaron jumped into the lift and pushed the button to take it down.

There were shouts from below, as the police started up the stairs. Then a long dying-fall scream from Ginny, as Zlot hurled her down the stairs into the ascending policemen, stopping them while he made his getaway.

"Oh no, you don't!" Belle's attention was still centred on Aaron. He was her personal adversary. "Oh no, you don't!" She clawed at the gate of the lift, dragging it open and tried to get into the lift with Aaron.

Aaron lashed out with the ebony walking-stick, slashing at her face, driving her back. As she advanced again, he switched his attack to her ankles, stabbing at them, tripping her.

Belle pitched forward, head and shoulders into the lift. The slowly, inexorably descending lift.

Amy screamed far longer than Belle did.

Chapter 15

The needlework was finished. Amy sat staring blankly at the completed picture in the frame. The man and woman faced outward, smiling serenely, faithful dog at their feet, fluffy Gainsborough clouds overhead, everything for the best in their best of all possible worlds.

Had life ever really been like that? At any time, for anyone, anywhere?

Aaron had wrenched open the lift doors at the next floor and leaped out—they had found traces of Belle's blood still staining his clothing later. He had met Zlot at the foot of the stairs and together they had charged down the remaining stairs to the ground floor. They had found a hapless citizen just trying to park his car as they emerged into the street. They had pulled him out of his car, flung him into the street and taken off in the stolen vehicle. A police car had given immediate chase and there had been a wild pursuit across London, ending only when the stolen car went out of control and plunged over the embankment into the river.

Inside the flat, the lighter fluid had splashed through Amy's hair on to the sofa, the sparks had kindled, the open door drew gusts of air down the tunnel of the hall-way. Only when the police tried to bring Amy back into the flat while waiting for the ambulance to arrive was the inferno discovered. By the time the fire brigade arrived, it was too late to save even the flat. Everything was finished.

When the police pulled the stolen car out of the river, it was empty. Days later, one of the bodies had surfaced. The clothes had indicated that it was Aaron. The fingerprints didn't help. Aaron had no "form" —he had never been caught before.

From the cocoon of her bandages, still in a state of shock, she had watched a patient inspector wrestle with her belief that Aaron was still alive. That she would know it—would *feel* it—if he were dead. That, in those last deadly moments, some invisible strand had spun out between them that would never be snapped while they were both alive. It was the reverse of undying love—but hate can be as eternal as love.

Aaron's mocking whistle, "Once in love with Amy . . ." had seemed to reverberate endlessly in her mind, haunting her through the unconscious, heavily sedated hours. Had she heard it or dreamed it? Or known instinctively that he was still alive somewhere, whistling that song under his breath to feed his hate . . . and waiting?

"You don't know of any birthmark?" The inspector was heavily patient, perhaps he didn't altogether disbelieve her instinct, he was nearing retirement and had probably seen too many inexplicable things. "Anything that might be useful for identification purposes?"

"His eyes," she said. They were his most remarkable feature. "His eyes were such a deep dark brown, almost black."

"His eyes . . ." The inspector sighed heavily. "The body had been in the water for quite a few days. As the conservationists keep telling us—" he sighed again— "the fish have come back to London's river."

Finished. Amy's hands plucked aimlessly at the rows of neat silk twists in her work-basket. A curious emptiness—a sense of loss, if any sense of loss could remain to her after having lost so much—possessed her. She had worked at this for so long that it had almost become a part of her, something that would continue as long as she did. There was a shadow of betrayal in the realization that this—her prop and mainstay—had deserted her. Now what would she do with the long days, the longer nights?

Perhaps—her stiff fingers lingered over a dark grey silk—she might shade the clouds a bit more . . . perhaps even turn them into dark storm-clouds, ready to burst and saturate the complacent couple sitting beneath them. No, she dismissed the idea, her hands moving away from the silks restlessly. The pattern was complete, there was nothing more that she could do.

Should she start another one? Listlessness pulled her back in her chair as though shrinking from the task. So much to do, so little really accomplished at the end of it.

Besides, she had no other design tonight. In the morning, Nurse Jellicoe would be glad to go out and buy her a fresh pattern, counting it as one more small link in the chain she imagined she was forging between them. She would be delighted to do so. But tonight . . .

The doorknob clicked. When Amy looked up, the door was already closing again, as though one of the nurses had just peeked in to make sure all was well.

All was not well. All would never be well again. Why did they bother to try to pretend otherwise?

She looked at her watch. The night staff would have been on duty for about an hour. Having settled fractious patients, soothed the frightened and administered the various medications called for, they would now be settling down themselves to the long routine of the night. They would not bother her—that battle had been decided a long time ago.

She heard the door open again. This time she did not look up. The door closed, leaving her with the sense of a presence still in the room. She looked up slowly.

The Yellow Lady stood in the doorway. They regarded each other for a long moment without speaking.

Amy's first thought was how deceiving appearances were. From above, the Yellow Lady had appeared to be smaller, frailer, more aristocratic. Foreshortened by distance and perspective, she had seemed delicate and graceful.

Looming in the doorway, ankles bulging outwards awkwardly over high heels, clutching the blonde mink around her with hands that seemed to be trying to burst out of the pale gloves, she looked grotesque. Even through the veil, it was apparent that she had applied make-up to the thickness and consistency of a mask.

She smiled and bright, distorted clown's lips parted only slightly to give a glimpse of teeth also smeared with the greasy lipstick.

Amy felt a faint pang of loss for what had obviously been a figment of her imagination: the gallant old woman who had come through many storms to find a quiet harbour in her mews house. This raddled harridan bore more resemblance to an unsuccessful streetwalker who had long ago lost her battle against the ravages of time and her trade. But why had she come here?

Still smiling, the Yellow Lady raised one hand to lift back the veil. It caught awkwardly on a stiff curl, tilting the whole blonde wig, giving her a rakish appearance quite at variance with the look in those dark brown eyes. The hatred in those dark brown—almost black—eyes.

"Hello, Amy," Aaron said.

"You're not surprised!" Aaron gave a grotesque imitation of a woman's pout.

"I knew you'd come," Amy said. Now that he was here, she felt no emotion at all.

"Clever of you." He tottered farther into the room with mincing unsteady steps, the heels wobbling under him. "Clever Amy—too clever by half!"

She didn't speak, just watched him advance.

"Don't touch that bell!"

She had not moved.

"That's better." He was beside her now, looking down at her. A miasma of cloying scent enveloped her. He had overdone the French perfume as well as the make-up.

"How did you get in here?" The question was familiar—too familiar—it had been asked before. Aaron was an expert at slipping through the net, eluding those who imagined they were sufficiently on guard against him.

"Nothing to it." He smirked, pleased that she had given him the opportunity to emphasize his cleverness. "People see what they expect to see. They're used to seeing the old bitch popping in and out of here. They didn't give me a second look."

"What have you done with her?" The question was torn from her—the Yellow Lady existed, not a figment of her own imagination. She was real—or had been.

"I'm glad you're interested," Aaron said. "I've brought you a little message from her. An invitation to fun and games at her place. We can't talk properly here. She . . . decided . . . she wouldn't mind lending us her place."

"You haven't hurt her?" Another innocent human being involved, brought to grief, because of her own initial stupidity.

"Hardly at all. She was quite reasonable . . . after a bit." He flexed his hands, a small tear appeared along the seam of one of the gloves.

"But how—" She broke off, finding that she already knew the answer. "The au pair," she said. "She gave you her key this afternoon—that was why she had to go through the window."

"That's right." He nodded approvingly. "She's not as bright as you are, Amy, but she's a lot more helpful."

Amy looked away, at the curtained window. Outside, the mews would still seem the same, except for the darkened house at the end. And no one would guess—

"I made friends with her," Aaron went on, "after I found out where you were. That wasn't hard—they didn't even try to hide the place they'd taken you. It was mentioned in all the papers."

"They thought you were dead," she said.

"But you didn't, did you, Amy?"

"No," she said. "Not even when they found the body."

"The body—" His face darkened. "That was Zlot! Zlot—dead! On account of you."

"Telle is dead because of you." She might as well not have spoken. He would recognize no counterclaim.

"Zlot! We grew up together. Friends all our lives. He even saved my life once, you know. When we were kids, playing on a bombsite. There was a landslide. I was buried. The others ran away, but Zlot didn't." Aaron's face was haunted, grim.

"Zlot stayed there and began digging. Even though there might be another landslide. He got me out, too. I remember his fingernails were all broken. He saved my life—but I couldn't save his. I couldn't do anything for him—"

"He was wearing your clothes," Amy said. Clearing that question seemed important.

"That's right." Aaron had regained some measure of control. "I got him out of the car—but it was too late. Not even the kiss of life worked. So I swam downriver and hid with him until it was dark. Then I changed clothes with him and trimmed his hair and cut off his beard. And—"

"And threw him back in the river."

"No! No, it wasn't like that. I *eased* him back—carefully and gently. I thought maybe the body would go out to sea. Zlot would have liked that—he always wanted to travel. But, if it didn't, and the police found it, then it was better that they thought they'd found me.

"In a way, it was like saving my life again—Zlot would have liked that, too.

"Then that left me free to look for you—and settle our score." The dark eyes brooded over her.

"I've been on the run. Do you know what that's like? No, you wouldn't. It was never having a place to stay, never having anyone you could trust, never having enough to eat—" He looked into space, lost for a moment, then his eyes returned to focus on her with deadly intensity.

"I'm going to eat tonight, though. There's food all ready. Lots of food. Oh—not for you. It's going to be a different kind of party for you. But you'll come, all the same, won't you, Amy? You can't refuse an invitation like this."

She had no sensation of fear, nor even the relief she'd expected to feel when Aaron finally came. There was only the same curious blankness that reaching the end of her needlework had brought her. The pattern was complete, she could not think beyond that.

"Get dressed, Amy," Aaron ordered softly. "The party is waiting for you."

"Kill me now," she said. "Here." But she knew it would not be that easy.

"Oh no, Amy. No." The grotesque lips parted again. "We aren't in any hurry, are we? This has been a long time coming. We wouldn't want to be interrupted."

She pushed aside the work-basket, the needlework frame—they had served their purpose. She wondered vaguely what would happen to the needlework. It would go to Harriet, she supposed, neatly packed by Nurse Jellicoe, and perhaps with an enclosed small sad note of sympathy—or apology.

"That's better," Aaron said. "We understand each other, don't we, Amy?"

Not looking at him, she crossed the room to the closet where she had watched Nurse Jellicoe hang what had been salvaged of her wardrobe. There was the dress she had been wearing when it happened—that was out. There were a couple of skirts and blouses—too complicated, her fingers were not supple enough yet to cope with buttons, hooks and eyes, zips. On a shelf at the side there was a navy blue sweater dress she had bought at a chain store during those barely-remembered early days of carefree shopping. That would do. She pulled it towards her, knowing that she had just chosen the dress for her own funeral.

It was a nice dress, it had looked well on her. She remembered vaguely a day when her mother, giggling, had quoted a slogan from her own girlhood to show that the generation gap was not as wide as it seemed: *"Live fast, die young, and make a good-looking corpse."*

She had really died several months ago, all that remained was to accomplish the formalities.

"Hurry along," Aaron said, readjusting his veil. "Sorry I can't wait to escort you—but that might attract attention. They're used to seeing her alone.

"I can depend on you, can't I—?" He moved closer. "Not to do anything silly? I'm not in this alone, you know. There are others—and they'd take care of everyone if anything happened to me. Not just you, you know. I don't suppose you give a damn about the old lady—you don't even know her—they'll start with her, if it gets tricky.

"But your sister is upstairs, isn't she? The old end of the alphabet in Room 414. *She* can't run away or—"

Amy closed her eyes. Ginny, lying helpless, unable to move. Unable even to shrink from hands reaching out for her throat, from a pillow descending over her face. If Aaron could get in, how much more certain that the au pair girl could walk in with some alleged message, or a bunch of flowers, and do as she pleased.

"I'll come," Amy said.

"I knew I could depend on you." The veil securely in place again, Aaron glanced in the mirror, straightened the wig, and seemed to approve of what he saw there.

"I'll say tatty-bye for now then." The back of a gloved

hand brushed her throat. "And we'll see you soon. You know the way, don't you? Turn left as you go outside this door and take the stairs at the end of the hallway. They'll lead you down to the ambulance entrance at the back. Make sure no one's watching when you slip out. That will bring you into the mews—and you can find the way from there, can't you?"

He paused in the doorway, fluttering his hand in a travesty of a woman's wave. The veil obscured the expression in his eyes, but she could feel them lingering on her face.

"Don't keep me waiting long," he said.

She dressed as quickly as her clumsy fingers would allow, even putting on lipstick. Then there was just one more thing she had to do.

Room 414. The door swung open beneath her touch. A night light was burning across the room. An inert form lay on the high hospital bed—impossible to tell whether she were asleep or awake.

"Ginny—" Amy crept closer. "Ginny, how are you?"

Only the eyes moved, sliding slowly sideways, shadowed and haunting. Then the lips moved, fighting to project a voice weak and creaking with disuse.

"Older," Ginny said.

PART TWO

Chapter 16

The au pair girl opened the door wearing the blonde mink coat. She stepped back quickly to let Amy in, closing the door immediately. Then she noticed Amy's eyes on the coat.

"Is nice." She stroked the fur voluptuously. "I keep. Aaron give."

"It doesn't belong to Aaron," Amy said. She had disliked the girl instinctively, just seeing her in the distance while looking down from the nursing home window. Facing her in the flesh, she knew that she had been right.

"*Everything*—" the contemptuous sweep of slate-grey eyes left no doubt of the au pair's meaning—"belong Aaron."

Losing interest in Amy, she turned away to preen before the pier glass. The beige wig, with hat and veiling still attached, lay in the corner of the console-table beneath the mirror, where it had obviously been tossed when Aaron tore it off as he entered.

"Amy—" Aaron appeared at the far end of the hall, rushing forward, his hands extended in a parody of a host. "*So* glad you could make it. How nice to see you here . . . at last." He took her by the shoulders, kissed first one cheek, then the other.

Cat-and-mouse. She didn't flinch—he would have enjoyed that too much.

111

"You've met Inga, I see."

Inga swung back her tangled mass of honey hair and pouted at herself in the mirror in acknowledgment of Aaron's words. She rolled up the collar of mink, pivoted, and surveyed herself from a fresh angle, half-closing her eyes, lost in some dream world of her own.

What else had Aaron promised her? Posing like a mannequin, did she see herself as a famous model, a film star? Did she imagine that Aaron had the money or influence to bring this about? Poor Inga—how long before the rude awakening came to her? *One more unfortunate . . .*

"I don't believe you know George." A door on the left had opened. The man standing there nodded, barely glancing at her. She was of no consequence to him, just another of Aaron's stupid birds.

"When do we eat?" he demanded. "You said we'd eat as soon as she got here."

She recognized him—everyone she had ever seen with Aaron was burned indelibly into her memory. He had been at the Soho club—the man Aaron had owed money to and had bought off with the name of a female victim he could con. What was Aaron paying with this time?

"What's she doing here?" George caught sight of Inga, still preening before the mirror. "Why isn't she in the kitchen?"

Inga whirled, eyes blazing. "I not serving girl!" The coat flew open, disclosing the bedraggled tank top and jeans underneath.

"That's right." Aaron moved quickly, stepping in between them, as though unsure of whether or not Inga might actually attack. "Inga is a lady, George. You ought to know that." Turning away from Inga, he winked at George. "Besides, we have someone else to do the donkey work now. Inga doesn't have to work any more."

"Is right." Inga nodded, mollified, and turned back to the mirror, clutching the mink around her again.

At least Aaron had moved away in order to calm his cohorts. Amy looked at them with indifference. There would be no point in looking to either of them for help, or even sympathy. They were too absorbed in their own preoccupations. Apart from which, they were Aaron's creatures—they would not protest at anything he chose to do.

But were there others? Amy looked beyond George, able to see only a corner of what appeared to be a lounge. It seemed to be empty. There was another room on the other side of the hall, straight ahead was undoubtedly the kitchen. A flight of stairs began just beyond the lounge door, leading to the three or four rooms upstairs. Beneath the closed-in stairs was another door where space had obviously been utilized for a closet, or perhaps a lavatory.

It was a jewel-box of a house, glowing within as it had seemed to glow down the dark mews when all the lights were on. The gleam of satin stripe in Regency wall hangings, the glow of gilt and shining brass, all were muted in the dim light of the single overhead bulb. Yet, there were other lights—a rose-shaded lamp on the console-table, an electrified candelabrum above the half-landing on the stairs—which remained dark. Was it because Aaron avoided bright lights, preferring to move in the shadows? Or was it simply because no one had given orders to light every light? The others would not have realized it was customary and Inga was too absorbed in her new image to give any thought to past routine.

What difference did it make? In a mews in which every curtain was drawn against the encroaching glare from the roof of the nursing home, who would notice that this house did not present its usual appearance? And who, noticing it, would construe any meaning from it?

And what of the Yellow Lady? Aaron had said she was not harmed, but who could trust Aaron? Stripped of her shimmering furs, her perky wig, was she lying somewhere —extinguished, as was the brightness of her home?

"Looking for someone?" Aaron's smile was cold, his parody of the perfect host wearing thin. "Who do you expect to see? Zlot? He's dead because of you—remember? A whole sweet little racket is finished—all because of you."

"I thought we were going to eat." George was truculent, uninterested in Aaron's reasons for vengeance. Uninterested, probably, in the vengeance itself.

"I, too." Inga crossed the hallway and swung open the opposite door. "We eat in here. Table is set." As Inga snapped a light on, Amy had a glimpse of gleaming rosewood, silver, and a Chinese gong within striking distance of a chair at the head of the table.

"Soon," Aaron said. "Very soon. No, not you, Amy. You don't eat. You're not hungry, anyway, are you? Not yet."

Amy didn't react. It was more important than ever now to give him no opening. Yet, why should she care? The best thing she could do for herself would be to provoke him into killing her instantly, rather than let him carry through whatever tortuous plan he had devised through these long months of waiting.

Perhaps it would come to that. Her mind weighed the idea and recognized it as valid. It could be put into action at any time. For the moment, her instincts were in command. And they held her suspended, curiously blank, waiting.

"Now what—?" Aaron frowned at her curiously, then snapped his fingers. "Of course, how remiss of me! Amy is a very well-brought-up little girl," he explained to the others. "She wants to pay her respects to her hostess. She wants to apologize because she hasn't brought anything with her. And she wants to ask if there is anything she can do to help. Don't you, Amy?"

"Yes," Amy said, the flicker of defiance surprising even herself.

"Don't worry—there's a lot you can do. And the old bitch will be glad of the help. She's never soiled her fingers with any work before—never known what it was to have a hard time—she'll be glad to have a lackey to give orders to again.

"This way—!" The sudden vicious jab in the small of her back sent her stumbling down the hallway to the kitchen door.

She caught herself at the doorway, holding on to the door jamb, reluctant to step inside. She did not want to see the Yellow Lady defeated—stripped of her finery, head bowed and sparse grey hairs unconcealed by the sheltering wig—at Aaron's mercy. Aaron, who was without mercy.

"Come on!" Aaron, impatient now, gave her another shove. "Hurry it up!"

Her first feeling was one of relief. The bowed head was as sleek as the wig and in the same tint of warm beige. The wig was intended to conceal nothing, then, except an inability to fit in a hairdressing appointment occasionally.

"Here, Ma," Aaron said. "I've brought company—somebody you can give orders to. Now that Inga's quit."

The bowed head lifted slowly, the face carefully expressionless, the eyes shuttered submissively. She was wearing a shabby yellow wool dressing-gown, clutched about her as though to compensate for the missing warmth of the mink Inga now flaunted. She did not look at Amy, nor did the lowered lids move to encompass Aaron, there was only the impression of a bright blue intentness, watchful, waiting. A faint fragrance of rose perfume surrounded her, subtler, lighter, than the scent Aaron had chosen for his masquerade. There was a bruise high on her cheekbone under her eye, and another on her chin.

"Wakey, wakey, Ma," Aaron said. "It's time to take care of your guests. You want to serve us a nice midnight supper, don't you? No trouble, is it? You and Inga got it all ready earlier, and now we've got little Amy to do all the running around for you. All you have to do is dish it up."

Silently, she got to her feet, still not looking at them, and Aaron nodded approvingly.

"That's better, Ma. I didn't think I'd have to persuade you again. You've learned your lesson, haven't you?" He didn't seem to expect an answer and he didn't get one.

"I'm loaning you out," he told Amy. "You do what she tells you. You'll do the fetching and carrying for her right now. I'll give you *my* orders . . . later."

Amy didn't answer, either.

"Right," he said. "I'm going back to my guests now. We'll have a few drinks in the lounge and then we'll go into the dining-room and you can serve us our supper there. We expect good service, remember, this is *our* party. When you hear my signal—jump to it!"

The light in the kitchen was the brightest in the house. It showed up the merciless crevices of Aaron's face. Had he always looked like that, or had the past months taken some toll of him, too? He had removed the make-up no more expertly than he had applied it and traces of cheap orangey foundation still streaked along the sides of his nostrils and in front of his ears. His mouth was blurred beyond its natural outlines by the remains of the dark lipstick which had lodged in his pores.

It was a clown's face. But there was nothing to laugh at about it.

"You've lost weight, Amy." He had been looking at her, too. "But not enough. We'll have to see what we can do about that—among other things—won't we? You've been having an easy time of it, lolling back, nurses waiting on you. You don't know what it is to be on the run, to have to—

"Sorry." He pulled himself up abruptly, with a perilous control that was more frightening than a descent into hysteria would have been. "My friends are waiting for me. We can discuss this again at our leisure—just you and I."

Amy watched him turn and walk back along the hallway, vaguely aware that the Yellow Lady was watching him, too. But when she turned, she found those sharp blue eyes studying her. There seemed to be an obscure satisfaction in their depths.

"You came," the Yellow Lady said. "So, you've some backbone left, after all."

"I'm sorry," Amy said. "I'm so terribly sorry about all this. That you've had to be caught in the middle of a—"

"I see." One corner of the wide mouth curved upwards in a lopsided smile. "So you came to help a poor old lady caught in a hopeless trap?"

"Not exactly that," Amy said. "I had to come. It wasn't just you. There's Ginny, too."

"Yes," the Yellow Lady said. "I know all about Ginny." She moved away from her rocking-chair and, for the first time, Amy could see into the far corner of the kitchen.

The scent of roses had not been due to perfume. There was a small living rose bush in a yellow wooden box some distance behind the rocking-chair. A tub of yellow roses.

"Sybilla!"

Chapter 17

"You're Sybilla!"

The bone structure, the lineaments of the face, the tilt of that bruised but undaunted chin—unmistakable now that they were face to face. Even looking down from her window on the stranger who lived in the mews, she had been reminded of Belle, thought that Belle would have aged like that woman. Her mind had been wiser than she in its unconscious linking of the two.

"And you're Amy!" Sybilla moved forward, taking the pink puffy fingers lightly and releasing them without pressure.

"I'm sorry—" Suddenly there was more, so much more, to apologize for than there had been when she'd thought Sybilla merely a stranger caught up in Aaron's revenge. She would have preferred a stranger, even on those terms—what was to come would have been easier to bear.

"Thank you. I'm sorry, too. But that's over and it can't be undone. All we can do is go on."

"That was what Belle said." Amy heard her voice shaking. In all this time, there had been no tears. She thought she had lost the capacity to cry.

"She was right," Sybilla said. "But you're here now. And *he's* here." Her hand moved along a piece of intricate plasterwork, seemed to find what it was seeking and lingered. "Now we can begin."

Amy frowned. "Begin—?"

All the lights in the house suddenly flickered and went out.

"What's happened?" Aaron's bellow of rage started at the end of the hall and grew louder as he came towards the kitchen again. "What have you done out here? Where are you?" A match sputtered and flared in the doorway.

"The lights," Sybilla said. "They've gone out."

"I can see they've gone out, you stupid cow. I don't need you to tell me that." But some of the anger was gone, he seemed mollified to find them still there. He had obviously suspected that they were planning to escape in the darkness.

"Perhaps there's a power failure." In the darkness, Sybilla sounded older, faintly querulous. "They're always having power failures—or strikes."

"No." Another match flared as George joined Aaron in the doorway. "The rest of the mews is okay—I've just checked."

"Must be a fuse." Aaron tossed the spent match on the floor and lit another. With reinforcements, he seemed more assured, almost amused. "You're death on fuses, aren't you, Amy?"

"Candles," Sybilla said vaguely. "There are candles in the dining-room."

"I know," George said. "Inga is lighting them. She'll be along with one in a—"

The screams ripped through the darkness like flashes of lightning—sudden, shattering, setting teeth on edge.

"Christ!" Aaron said. "*Now* what?"

"Aarun, Aarun!" Inga came hurtling towards them, her candle extinguished by the rush of her headlong flight. Still screaming, sobbing, incomprehensible, she threw herself into his unwilling arms.

"Icy die!" she sobbed. "Icy die!"

Amy was aware of a barely discernible movement by Sybilla. Abruptly, the electricity came back on. In the blaze of light, Inga looked more slatternly than ever. Even the mink had acquired some of her grubbiness, a splash of candle wax matted on the front, a dusting of powder on the collar.

"What is it?" Aaron shook her impatiently. "What's the matter with you?"

Inga shook her head, still babbling. Her command of English obviously unequal to her experience, she had lapsed into some Scandinavian language.

"What's going on here?" Aaron turned to Sybilla suspiciously. "What's the matter with Inga?"

"Matter?" Sybilla drew herself up, no longer bothering to try to hide the contempt in her eyes. "She is lazy, incompetent and hysterical." She spoke coldly, an employer refusing to give references. "I'm surprised you haven't discovered that before now."

Aaron's hand twitched. He moved towards Sybilla. Before he reached her, Inga began screaming again. He whirled and slapped her across the face instead.

"Shut up!" he ordered. "You, too!" He glared at Sybilla.

"She does not talk of me that way!" Inga whimpered. The immediate insult seemed to have steadied her, as though it were something she was able to cope with. "I am work here. I am work here long."

"That's right, Ma," Aaron said. "If she's so bad, I'm surprised you didn't sack her."

Sybilla shrugged. "She suited my purpose," she said. "She can consider herself 'sacked' now, however."

"That's rich, coming from you, Ma," Aaron sneered at her. "You're in no position to sack anybody. Can't you get that into your head? *I'm* giving the orders now."

Sybilla shrugged again. Belatedly, she lowered her

eyelids. Had Aaron caught that sudden blaze of hostility, he might not have been able to delude himself that he had subdued her, that orders were his to give.

But Aaron was occupied with Inga, trying to coax her out of the sulking fit he had brought on. "There, you're better now, aren't you? Take a deep breath and speak English. What was the matter?"

Inga pouted and drew the mink closer around her. Noticing that she still held the candle, she flung it from her pettishly. It rolled across the floor and came to rest against Amy's feet. Amy stooped and picked it up automatically.

"Come on," Aaron said. "What frightened you into fits?"

"I not feel good." Inga shivered.

"You had a pain, you mean?" Aaron was plainly disbelieving. "A pain made you scream like that?"

"My face hurt." Inga raised a hand to her cheek. "You hit." Her chin thrust forward mutinously. "I not feel good."

"Forget that!" Aaron's fist clenched, unseen by Inga. Slowly he unclenched it. "You've had a hard day." The words were sympathetic, the voice was not. "You're tired. You're hungry. We'll have something to eat now and talk about it later. All right?"

George had already disappeared. Perhaps gauging Aaron's mood when Inga had begun to add rebellion to hysteria, he had backed quietly away, then turned and melted silently down the hallway.

Inga tossed her head and allowed herself to be ushered into the hallway, Aaron still making solicitous noises. He must still need her, then, for some further reasons of his own. And, from the hints she had had, Amy did not find it difficult to guess at those reasons. Undoubtedly, through Inga, Aaron intended to meet other au pairs who could be paid or persuaded to deliver up their employers' valuables to him.

Also without doubt he intended to make the mews house his operational headquarters for quite some time. It would be safe, quiet, unsuspected. With Inga making occasional strategic appearances on dark days, or at night, wearing the blonde mink, no one would realize anything was wrong. He could carry out his macabre plans without hindrance.

His plans included her, Amy realized. From the hints he had dropped, she knew that he planned to keep her prisoner, starve her slowly, while forcing her to serve ever more elaborate meals. That was just one of the things he had planned for her. What were the others? And what did he intend for Sybilla?

"We'll eat now!" His face was black with suppressed rage when he turned to hurl the order at them. "So get a move on!" His footsteps faded away in a furious tattoo.

Sybilla was smiling.

"I'd light that candle, if I were you," she told Amy. "There are two more—and candlesticks—in the drawer beside the sink. Take them out and light them, please. Once the electricity begins misbehaving, it usually continues to do so."

In all the long nights she had gazed into the mews from her window, Amy had never seen any sign of the electricity being anything less than perfect in the house at the end of the mews. But Sybilla must have the memory of other nights, other years, behind her request.

Amy found the candles, fitted them into the little pottery holders, and hesitated.

"The matches are in the drawer, too." Sybilla's voice was calm and firm, expecting obedience. Yet she must know something of the struggle going on.

"I see them," Amy said. Twice she reached for the little yellow box and twice her fingers flinched away involuntarily, refusing to close around it.

She braced herself, aware of Sybilla watching, waiting. This time her fingers grasped the box, opened it, fumbled for a match. It didn't ignite on the first attempt, but she slashed it at the striking surface again and this time it did.

She couldn't control the shaking, but she managed to keep the flame close enough to the wick for it to catch, then lit the second candle before the match went out. Resolutely, she struck another match to light the candle Inga had thrown, and stood back, feeling a sense of wonder at her own accomplishment. Sybilla had been right—there *was* some backbone still left. Furthermore, it was strengthening by the minute.

She didn't follow that line of thought any farther. For the moment, that was far enough. That—and the knowledge that there was a vista—a possibility—opening out ahead. She blew out the guttering match quickly.

Behind her, she heard Sybilla's faint breath of relief. Then, from down the hall, the crash of reverberating brass—someone had struck the Chinese gong in the dining-room.

Quickly, Sybilla sprang into a flurry of activity, opening the fridge, removing dishes, bottles and ramekins. "Take this down to them first—it will keep them occupied." She thrust a carafe of chilled white wine into Amy's hands.

There had been something Amy had intended to say, but it would have to wait. Any hesitation would bring Aaron charging down the hallway again to confront them. He mustn't guess that any sort of scheme was beginning to form in her mind.

"Amy—" She turned in the doorway. Sybilla was standing beside the oven, having just transferred the ramekins into it.

"Amy—whatever happens—whatever you see—don't do anything. Don't speak, don't move. Don't react at all."

"I know," she said. She didn't need Sybilla's warning. Whatever Aaron said or did, she would not allow him to provoke her into any display of emotion.

"I don't believe you do," Sybilla said.

Chapter 18

The remaining candles were aglow in the centre of the gleaming rosewood table. The electric lights were on as well and, once inside the room, Amy could see the side-board against the inner wall.

Not looking at Aaron or the others, she fitted the carafe into a wood-and-pierced-silver coaster and brought it over to the table, realizing what Sybilla had been hinting at.

An open suitcase covered half the sideboard, packed with gold and silver: a jumble of cutlery, jewellery, candelabra, salvers, picture frames, ornaments—waiting to be closed and taken away. She had known that she would never leave this house alive. Now she knew that Aaron did not intend Sybilla to survive, either.

Inga seemed more apprehensive in here than she had in the kitchen. She had slipped her arms out of the sleeves, but was still huddled into the mink, elbows resting on the table, hands plucking restlessly at the edges of the coat, she kept darting quick sly glances around the room, her eyes returning to the doorway repeatedly, swiftly, as though expecting to surprise an intruder there. But they were the intruders in this house.

George brightened and reached for the wine as Amy set it down, but Aaron rapped his knuckles sharply.

"Don't be ignorant," he said. "The waitress takes care of that. Amy will pour it for us, won't you, Amy? But none for you, Amy. You don't mind, do you, Amy? You're not thirsty, are you, Amy? Not yet."

Silently, she filled the glasses, knowing that Aaron was pleased to observe the shaking of her hand. But he was wrong. She wasn't frightened. It was the unaccustomed weight of the carafe in a hand which had manipulated nothing heavier than needle and thread for months. And also, she identified with a fresh sense of wonder, it was the beginning of a deep anger. She had little interest in her own fate, but she discovered that she cared about Sybilla's. It was too much that Aaron should be allowed to lop off both branch and root of the same family tree.

"Clumsy, Amy, very clumsy." Aaron looked at the drops of wine on the table.

She kept her eyelids lowered, aware that new life must be blazing in her eyes, along with a new resolution. Aaron must not be put on his guard, he was relaxed now, certain that he had the situation in hand. He must be allowed to continue to think that, while she—while she began to think.

"I wish food," Inga said. That wish had not prevented her from draining her glass. She thrust it imperiously at Amy and Amy filled it again.

"All right," Aaron ordered. "Go get the food!" He picked up the padded hammer, weighing it judiciously in his hand, as though deciding whether to strike her or the gong.

Amy set the wine back on the table and withdrew without haste and without hesitancy, not betraying how glad she was to get away. She could sense that Aaron found her behaviour unsatisfactory, perhaps he had expected pleading or tears. He would never see either from her, he might be beginning to suspect that now. She could feel his eyes on her as she left the room.

*　　*　　*

For one startled moment, she thought she heard voices coming from the kitchen as she approached. But it must have been the echoes of a conversation started in the dining-room behind her. Acoustics were odd phenomena, especially in unfamiliar houses.

Sybilla was staring pensively into space when Amy entered the kitchen. The aroma of fish and sizzling cheese merged with the scent of beeswax, an empty tray waited on the table.

Amy glanced upwards at the light bulb, there was no sign of any further flickering. She could only hope that Sybilla was right. On that, they must base their plans.

"Sybilla," she spoke softly. (If voices could carry down the hall to the kitchen, they might travel in reverse as well.) "Sybilla, where's the telephone?"

"Telephone? Don't bother about that," Sybilla said. "They cut the wires hours ago." She seemed to find something amusing in the thought.

Amy relinquished the idea almost gladly. It hadn't been a very good one. Telephone dials are noisy, there were too many listening ears to catch the spinning sound. It would have been hard to dial in darkness—even 999 could be too easily misdialled, and there would not have been a second chance.

"Listen, then, Sybilla," she said. "It's me he's after. You're just incidental—he doesn't even know who you are, does he—?"

Sybilla shook her head. "Not yet."

"Then, next time the lights go out, you can get away. I'll stay here, make sure he knows I'm still here, and he won't even think about you. You can slip out the back door—"

"No." Sybilla shook her head again. "They've locked the back door and taken the key. And they've nailed the ground floor windows shut." Her voice clotted with amusement. "They've been very busy."

"Then we can't get out." Her disappointment was not for herself.

"Neither can they," Sybilla said.

"Perhaps we could signal from the window with a candle." Amy still pursued the disappearing fragment of her train of thought.

"Signal to whom?" Sybilla asked.

"The police—" Before the polite disbelief in those bright blue eyes, Amy faltered, then tried to explain. "If they—when they discover I'm missing from the nursing home, they'll wonder where I've gone. It—it might not be until morning, when the policewoman comes back on duty, but if—if any of the staff remember anything unusual—like signalling—coming from here during the night, she might put two and two together and send someone to investigate." If only Policewoman Jellicoe *would* send someone else, and not decide to come along all alone and check things out for herself.

"What an absurd idea," Sybilla said. "Whatever makes you think the police are the least interested in what you do?"

"You don't understand," Amy said. "They've been waiting to trap Aaron. I told them I believed he was still alive and that he'd come after me. That's why they've kept me for so long in that nursing home, under surveillance. I was a—a Judas goat—to lure Aaron into their trap."

"I see." That, too, seemed to amuse Sybilla. Amy wondered if she had lost her grasp of the situation—she could not possibly smile if she realized how serious it was. "But I'm afraid you're mistaken. The police believed Aaron dead—the body they recovered from the river had enough identification on it to give them the right to assume that."

"But they've been keeping me—"

"I know everyone thinks our police are wonderful,"

Sybilla said, "but you seem to believe that they have unlimited financial resources, endless time, and no other cases to work on. No." She shook her head with finality. "So far as the police are concerned, the case is closed. It was closed months ago when they found that body."

"Then—" Amy had not realized how much she had begun to hope again until the black despair engulfed her. "Then, the police won't be coming. We can't look to them for help."

"I should hope not," Sybilla said. "What would we want the police here for?"

"What—?" Amy could not finish. Sybilla must be mad. Too many family tragedies must have unhinged her, and the death of a favourite granddaughter must have been the final straw.

"They'd be in the way," Sybilla said coldly. "Furthermore, they would undoubtedly insist on arresting your erstwhile friend and taking him to prison. I should find that extremely tiresome of them."

"But prison is where he belongs," Amy said faintly.

"Do you think so?" Sybilla wasn't smiling now. "Do you honestly think so?"

"But—" Amy hesitated. Something had changed in Sybilla's face. Unnoticed muscles had moved, hardened, brought new tautness to her jaw, coldness to her eyes. Sybilla was not mad—or, if so, she was still a force to be reckoned with.

"You were right about one thing," Sybilla said, her voice, too, was distant, had the new coldness. "You *have* been used as the stalking lamb—the Judas goat, if you prefer. But I'm the one who has used you.

"You see, I felt you were right when you insisted that Aaron was still alive. While you were still unconscious, your nurse heard someone whistling a tune somewhere outside. She recognized it as 'Once In Love With Amy' and saw the effect it had on you. It frightened her, too, but when she went to the door and looked out, she could see no one. She reported it to the police, but they discounted it. *I*, however, believed what the police could not. And so, I waited."

"Waited . . ." Amy repeated haplessly, mesmerized by this new Sybilla. Awed, but not afraid. For the first time, it occurred to her that Sybilla might be more than a match for Aaron. That Aaron was no longer the moving spirit, but had become the pawn in some game he was not even aware of.

"I found this house," Sybilla said. "It suited my purpose admirably. *That's* why you were in that particular nursing home—it's no better and no worse than dozens of others all over London and the Home Counties.

"Yes—" she answered the unspoken question. "I'm the one who has been paying the bills for you and your sister. I have also kept in touch with your family, trying to keep them from worrying unduly—and also dissuading them from coming over here.

"I would ask you to believe—" for a moment her face softened with warmth—"it was not *solely* to use you. At least part of it was because you were a guest—of our country and our family—and because Belle betrayed our laws of hospitality. She should not have left you to your own devices immediately upon arrival. She should have stayed with you, or else brought you North with her."

"Oh no," Amy whispered. "It was *my* fault—only mine." Yet, even as she spoke, she felt a further faint lightening of her spirit. It had never occurred to her that any blame at all could accrue to Belle for what had happened.

"Belle should have known better," Sybilla pronounced judgment. "Nevertheless—" her voice frosted again—"she did not deserve what happened to her, and neither did you. You were both young, still unformed. You had a lot to learn, but the lessons should not have been so hard, so

final. They aren't, with most women. You were exception-
ally unlucky."

"I was stupid," Amy said bitterly. "Just plain stupid.
Too stupid to live—" She broke off, she was still alive. It
was Belle who had paid the price for Amy's stupidity. That
was what she could not live with.

"The price was too high—" Sybilla might have been
reading her mind—"to be shrugged off as 'just one of
those things.' Too many of you paid it—are still paying it.
Everyone paid except Aaron. It's time he settled his
account."

"Then let's think of a way we can contact the police,"
Amy said urgently, still trying to break through to some
inner core where Sybilla—the real Sybilla, Belle's beloved
Gran'mère—dwelt. "The police can arrest him and—"

"And that's all they can do," Sybilla said. "That's not
enough. A trial, a bit of unpleasantness, a few years in
jail—plenty of time off for good behaviour—he'll be out to
prey upon the world again in a few years. The police do
the best they can but, basically, their hands are tied. They
can't mete out enough punishment—or the right kind of
punishment. They're useless, for my purpose. There'll be
time enough for the police later."

My purpose. Sybilla kept using those words.

"What *is* your purpose?" Amy asked.

Sybilla looked above and beyond her, a cold implacable light in her face.

"The creature is an animal," she said. "A mad dog,
unfit for human society. Because of him, my granddaughter died—and died horribly.

"I intend to deal with him as I would deal with any
mad dog. I intend to destroy him."

Chapter 19

The Chinese gong sounded from the dining-room, its imperative summons reverberating through the air. The echo had hardly died away when a fresh boom sounded, then another. Aaron was going to continue crashing the hammer against the gong until someone came. He was enjoying himself, playing lord and master.

"Yes, we're coming," Sybilla said, under her breath. "Oh, we're coming!" She shrugged off the yellow wool dressing-gown abruptly, tossing it over the arm of the rocking-chair where it lay like a discarded cocoon. Beneath it, she was wearing the sort of trouser-suit that one associated with Chinese peasant women, except that this was in a rich iridescent brocade, of a green so dark it was nearly black, with gold threads glinting through it, catching the light when she moved. From the mandarin collar to trousers as tapered and close-fitting as the sleeves, there was not a spare inch of material which might catch on anything or otherwise impede her movements. For all its beauty, it was a curiously practical, businesslike outfit. It occurred to Amy that Sybilla was now stripped for action.

"I'll take the tray—you couldn't manage it." Sybilla swiftly transferred the steaming ramekins from the oven to the waiting tray. The brocade rippled with her movements, supple as a snakeskin. Wasn't it in Oriental legends that the snake represented eternal wisdom?

"You can take this." Two halves of a French loaf, cut at intervals and brushed with garlic butter, had also been in the oven. Sybilla tossed them into a wicker basket and handed it to Amy. "Let me go first—and keep your mouth shut."

Amy followed Sybilla down the hallway. Sybilla's speed increased as she neared the dining-room, taking little tottering steps, as though the tray were too heavy for her. Amy felt guilty, but knew that she could not have managed the tray herself. Sybilla was right—it would have been too much for her. Of course, that was what Aaron had intended.

"What kept you?" Aaron demanded. "I want action and I want it fast when I hit that gong."

"Oh!" Sybilla slammed the tray down on the table with a gasp of distress.

"You're getting past it, Ma." Aaron seemed obscurely satisfied by her display of weakness. "Why didn't you let Amy bring that? I told you she'd do everything from now on."

"It would have taken her two trips." Sybilla's voice was again thin and faintly querulous, she had donned fragility like a cloak. "You were hungry. In a hurry."

"That's right! You're right!" Aaron laughed hugely. "I got you trained in a hurry, didn't I, Ma? You know what's good for you."

Amy had been holding her breath but, incredibly, it seemed that Sybilla had brought it off successfully. Intent on the fragrant food, watching Aaron, none of them had noticed.

Sybilla's carefully aimed gasp of distress had blown out one of the candles.

"We eat now." Inga leaned across the table and snatched a ramekin from the tray. "I do bread." She glared at them as though someone had challenged the statement. "Where is bread?"

"Here." Amy brought it forward, depositing the wicker basket on the table beside the tray. Once again, Inga snatched greedily.

"Carried that in all by yourself, did you?" Aaron grinned sarcastically. "You're not going to put yourself out to be any help to a poor old lady, are you?"

Aaron was concentrating on her, Inga concentrating on food. George glanced at Aaron uneasily, then helped himself to a ramekin and tore off a piece of bread. No one was paying any attention to Sybilla.

Out of the corner of her eye, Amy saw Sybilla move. Swift as a striking serpent, her hand lashed out—and another candle was extinguished.

"You'll have to do better than that, Amy," Aaron said. "You aren't pulling your weight around here."

"I will," Amy said. She must keep Aaron's attention centred upon herself, he must not look at Sybilla.

"Here." Fumbling awkwardly, Amy managed to grasp the handle of the remaining ramekin and set it in front of Aaron.

"That's better." He leaned back, pleased. "I think you may be beginning to learn your lesson, too. Not half as much as you're going to learn—but it's a start."

Amy backed away, daring now to glance at Sybilla, who was slumped submissively by the door, as though awaiting dismissal. In the bright flood of light from the chandelier, it was not immediately noticeable that all the candles were now out.

"Right!" Aaron seemed to have been going to say more, but the teasing fragrance wafting up from the ramekin distracted him. He reached for a chunk of garlic bread and waved them away.

"Just one thing, Ma—" They were nearly out of the

door when his voice halted them. "Let *her* carry the next course in by herself. You understand?"

"All right," Sybilla quavered. "All right."

In the kitchen, Sybilla attacked the cold chicken with a suppressed fury that sent shreds of skin and meat flying in all directions. If Aaron could have seen her at this moment, he would not have felt so secure in his dominance of the situation—not while Sybilla could wield a carving knife like that. Even the odds of three-to-one wouldn't be such a comfort to him.

The odds, Amy paused and corrected herself, of *three-to-two.* Even though her stiff fingers would be powerless to grasp and use a knife to any effect, there must be something she could do. There *had* to be something she could do, when the time came.

The time . . . but there were two times looming up in the immediate future: Aaron's time and Sybilla's time. Which would come first?

"Sybilla—" It was unlikely that they could hear her in the dining-room, but she whispered anyway. "Sybilla, what are you going to *do*?"

"Toss the salad," Sybilla commanded crisply, ignoring her question. "You'll find it in the refrigerator. The dressing is in the bottle beside the bowl."

"Sybilla—" Automatically, she fetched the bowl from the fridge, making a second trip for the bottle of dressing. She still felt safer carrying anything of any weight or size with both hands.

"This side of the table," Sybilla directed absently. She was carving with cold precision now, the fury of her first onslaught abated.

Obediently, Amy pushed bowl and bottle across the table and walked round to join Sybilla. They were both on the far side, the width of the table between them and the door.

"Sybilla—" Despite Sybilla's implacable face, she had to make the effort. "Sybilla, let's try to get the police. You can't do anything—you musn't. It—he—isn't worth it."

"I'm old." Sybilla faced her abruptly, the harsh kitchen light accentuating the many fine lines and hollows in the saffron-shaded face attesting the truth of her statement. "Never mind how old. I've lived a long life and a full one. Some of it has been good—very good—and some of it has been bad—very bad. But I intend to live it to the end."

"The end could be prison." Amy felt that she might have been talking to some carved Buddha with as much effect. Sybilla didn't seem to know what she was trying to say. Or perhaps Sybilla just didn't care. "Even—hanging."

"I hardly think so." Once again, Sybilla was amused. "Isn't there a saying in your country—something about a rich man never having gone to the electric chair? We like to think of our system as above influence but, basically, the same holds true. In any case, the death penalty has been abolished. That's why—" her face hardened again—"I shall take care of Aaron myself."

"They'll still arrest you," Amy protested. "They'll still send you to prison—"

"It won't be my first experience of it," Sybilla reminded her. "And I believe any English prison would seem like a holiday hotel after a Japanese concentration camp."

"But—"

"In any case, I doubt if it would come to that. Remember these people broke into my home, held me captive—" She turned her head slightly, so that the bruises loomed large and dark. "They used violence. English courts have never liked that sort of thing, and there's been an increasing reaction against it lately."

"You shouldn't have let him hurt you—"

"He wouldn't have believed it if I'd given in too easily," Sybilla said. "And it will be as well to have a few marks to show—afterwards."

"But if you deliberately lured him here—" Amy felt faintly dizzy at the way Sybilla was twisting the facts into her own representation of the truth. Which *was* true and yet, at the same time, so very far from the truth. "And you've just admitted you did—"

"Are *you* going to tell the police that?"

"No," Amy decided. She concentrated painfully on keeping her grasp on the salad fork and spoon, carefully turning the lettuce leaves over and over. Trying not to remember that Belle, too, had been so sure of herself, that Belle had made something of the same affirmative statement of life—just before she clashed with Aaron.

"In any case," Sybilla abruptly answered a still-unspoken argument, "it wouldn't come to that. Not prison. There are so many competent and discreet private nursing homes, so many specialists who would testify to the belated effects of a long spell in a prison camp.

"And—" she smiled suddenly again—"I suspect one might be rather surprised at the number of dear friends who would willingly take the witness stand and swear in all sincerity that they believe one to have been quietly mad as a hatter for years."

Amy could not repress an answering smile.

"No," Sybilla concluded, "it wouldn't come to prison. A suite of one's own in a well-run and expensive sanatorium, quite possibly. I've known worse—much worse. There's one which already contains a couple of old friends—on their better days, we might even get a good bridge game going. It wouldn't be so bad. And I'd count it worth the price—remember that."

"He isn't worth it," Amy protested again. The thought of her dauntless Yellow Lady—Sybilla—locked away, shut up in what was a prison in all but name, overwhelmed her. It could not be allowed to happen.

Which meant that something must be done to prevent it. *She* must do something. But what?

Chapter 20

Abrupt as a scream for help, the imperious summons of the brass gong sounded again. This time there was no pause between strokes for effect. Again and again, the gong reverberated, filling the house with a clamour that must surely be hitherto unknown to it.

"Yes." Sybilla tipped back her sleeve to peer at the thin gold wafer on her wrist. "Yes, I think it *is* time." She crossed to the patch of fancy plasterwork on the farther wall and stretched out her hand.

"Stay where you are," she ordered.

This time Amy was prepared for the sudden swoop of blackness. The kitchen candles were still alight and their dim glow seemed to increase as if their flames swelled to combat the dark. It was just, she told herself, that her eyes were accustoming themselves to the different lighting.

Sybilla came back to the table, picked up the knife again and went on carving as though nothing had happened. Following her cue, Amy poured a bit more dressing over the salad and went on tossing it. Neither of them spoke.

There were no candles lit in the dining-room. The shouts and confusion rang through the hall. There was a clatter of tableware, the crash of a breaking dish or glass. Then the gong began to boom in a mad syncopated rhythm.

"Stay here," Sybilla said, not moving.

After a time, they heard the sound of someone blundering along the passage, thudding against unfamiliar walls. Then Aaron stumbled into the kitchen, blinking against the brightness of the candles after the pitch black of the rest of the house.

"You're here," he said. He seemed relieved, as though he had expected to find his birds had flown.

"Where else would I be?" Sybilla kept carving, the light glinted along the sharp blade. "This is *my* house."

"That's right, Ma." He glared at her malevolently. "And you do all right for yourself, don't you? I see *you've* got candles. What happened to ours?"

Sybilla shrugged. A gleam of light flashed along the knife blade.

"Right." Aaron eyed the blade uneasily. "Just stay right where you are." He lunged forward, captured a candle from the table, and backed away.

"All right, Ma," he said. "I'll take that knife before I go. No—" as Sybilla moved—"don't hand it to me. I wasn't born yesterday. Put it down on the table—handle towards me. That's it."

As Sybilla complied, he edged forward and caught up the knife. "That's better." His swagger was returning. With light and a weapon, he was himself again.

"Why don't you take the chicken, too?" Sybilla held out the platter. "It's all ready."

"Don't get funny, Ma." Aaron moved away. "Just wait here until I signal, and *then* you can bring in the chicken. After we finish eating, George and I will take a look at your fuse box. You must have a loose connection somewhere."

"That will be very helpful." Sybilla smiled as he left the room and it was not a pleasant smile.

When the gong sounded this time there seemed a different tone to it, not quite so commanding, nor reverberating for so long.

"You take the food." Sybilla juggled the empty plates in one hand, a bottle of wine and the lighted candle in the other. As she turned at the doorway she took the curve too sharply and the bottle clanked against the door jamb, but did not break.

Amy followed more slowly, the platter of chicken balanced on top of the bowl of salad, which she was holding with both hands. She was conscious of the unaccustomed physical strain on her muscles, but gradually becoming conscious also that she was stronger than she had realized. Perhaps the doctor had been right when he had told her impatiently that she had recovered everything except the will to live.

Sybilla had drawn the cork in the kitchen, now she splashed wine into the empty glasses as soon as she had put down the plates. Almost ostentatiously, she filled the plates with chicken and salad and passed them round.

Aaron watched her suspiciously, as though he distrusted such docility but could not fault it.

"More wine!" Inga took the service as her due, holding out her glass imperiously. If she had not had quite a bit already perhaps the sudden flinty look in Sybilla's eyes might have given her pause. As it was, she waited for the glass to be filled, then drank from it greedily, spilling some of it on the mink.

The candles made a bright pool of light in the centre of the table, which eddied out to a soft blurring of vision in the farther corners of the room. Something seemed vaguely different about the room, a difference that could not solely be accounted for by the change in lighting. Amy glanced around uneasily.

Abruptly, the overhead lights came on again, flooding the room with a brilliance that set them all blinking. They froze like statues, then Aaron laughed.

"That's better," he said. "This is a crazy house, you've

got, Ma. The electricity—" He broke off, staring at something behind them.

Amy turned slowly, trying to make the movement inconspicuous, sensing that anything that attracted Aaron's attention now would draw his spite, as well. He was back in that dangerous mood again. But what had—

Then she saw it. Rather, *didn't* see it. The suitcase which had been on the sideboard and piled with valuables was missing.

"Right!" Aaron pushed his chair, glaring at George and Inga. "What do you think you're playing at? I want that back—and I want it *now!*"

"Huh?" George lifted his head from his plate. "What's the matter with you?"

"The stuff!" Aaron pointed to the empty sideboard. "Where is it?"

"How do I know?"

"Don't give me that! It was here before the lights went out. Where is it?"

"Yeah," George stood up slowly, challengingly. "Where is it?"

"You were here—both of you—alone—while I went to get a candle." Aaron's head moved from side to side, like an animal's, scenting danger, trying to track its source.

"And you went off—all by yourself," George said. "Leaving Inga and me here in the dark. We couldn't see a thing. You could have gone anywhere. You could have done anything."

Inga watched them impassively, drops of wine glinted like anaemic blood against the blonde mink.

"What have you got to say for yourself?" Aaron turned on her. "You were here. You could have done it."

"I do not move." She faced him haughtily. "I not see in dark."

"Somebody can see too much." Aaron moved away from the table, crouched to look underneath, straightened

again and went to block the doorway, glaring at them all.
"You can't have gone far with it," he addressed them all
impartially. "It must still be here in the house."

"That's right." George turned. "Suppose we all go
and look for it—together."

"Ja." Inga got up and came round the table, greed of
a different sort motivating her. "Is right."

"Together? Wait a minute," Aaron said. "We can't
leave these two alone for long. They might—"

"Why not?" George was truculent now. "They can't
get out. You locked both doors, didn't you?"

"The keys are still in my pocket. But—" Aaron seemed
to notice abruptly that he had been forced into a defensive
position. "It's one of you—it's *got* to be. I went straight
down to the kitchen. Didn't I?" Incredibly, he appealed to
Sybilla.

She ignored him.

"Didn't I?" he demanded.

"Didn't you what?" She raised an eyebrow.

"Didn't I come down to the kitchen as soon as the
light went out? For a candle." He glared at her in baffle-
ment. "Haven't you been paying any attention?"

"Why should I concern myself with your petty quar-
rels?" Her eloquent shrug dismissed them as something
beneath her notice, something less than human. "It has
always been my understanding that thieves have a habit of
falling out."

Her head ricocheted against the door jamb from the
violence of Aaron's slap.

"Leave her alone!" Amy moved forward.

"Ja." Inga glanced at Sybilla in momentary perilous
partisanship. "Me also he hit."

"I'll hit you again, you stupid cow, if you don't shut
up!" It was a mistake and he was instantly aware of it. His
face smoothed, took on more ingratiating lines.

"Come on, you're playing games with me." He laughed unconvincingly. "Put it back and we'll forget about it."

"Suppose *you* put it back," George said.

"You want to play it that way?" Aaron's face was grim. "Right! We'll play it that way. Come on, we'll search the whole bleeding house!"

"What about them?" This time it was George who was uneasy. He indicated Amy and Sybilla with a wave of his hand.

"What about them? Let them come with us." Aaron turned and they all followed him across the hall and into the living-room. Inga slipped her arms back into the sleeves and drew the mink around her, as though armouring herself against the unknown.

Aaron and George surged through the room, tossing sofa cushions to the floor, upturning chairs, opening and ransacking chests. Sybilla stood impassive in the doorway with Amy, watching them.

"Is not here." Inga flapped in their wake, watching the growing disorder with the concern of one who had had to clean the room too many times in the past, who was still perhaps not quite able to believe that she would not have to undo all traces of disruption after this.

"Right." Aaron straightened from peering beneath the last possible hiding-place. "Maybe it isn't. But you didn't have time to get far—and I was in the kitchen."

"So *you* say," George muttered.

"Yes, *I* say so." Aaron glared at him. "Right! That's it for down here. Upstairs everyone!"

How could Sybilla stay so unconcerned as she watched them tear her home apart? She looked as calm and unruffled as though the whole thing had no earthly connection with herself. Was it because she had already mentally bid goodbye to the treasures she had lost—or because she knew what had happened to them? Yet, how could she? She had been in the kitchen, not out of sight for one second during the time when they must have disappeared.

Oddly enough, it was Inga who appeared to be getting into a state about it. Inga who uttered increasing cries of distress as they tore through the upstairs room; who retrieved pillows from the floor and replaced them on the beds; who, finally, looked older and more haggard as they finished their search and trooped downstairs again.

Sybilla remained untouched by it all. Her face under such careful control that Amy suspected she was hiding some private amusement again. Somehow, they were all playing into her hands.

"It's here somewhere—it's *got* to be." Aaron and George glared at each other like adversaries.

"That's what *I* think," George said. "That's why I want to search the kitchen next."

"I told you—*I* was in the kitchen."

"Yeah," George said. "That's what I mean."

Aaron would make him pay for that—later. The threat gleamed in Aaron's narrowed eyes. "Right," he said, "the kitchen—you *could* have slipped past me in the dark."

While they searched, Inga confined her examination to the refrigerator, her interest obviously waning. The missing silver seemed to have lost reality for her, it was less than the opulent mink that swathed her.

"We finish eat," she suggested, trailing a stranded cuff into the cream jug as she rummaged at the back of a shelf.

"Maybe we will." Aaron straightened from inspecting a cupboard under the sink, holding a variety of sharp-edged tools he was confiscating lest they be turned into weapons. "What's for pud, Ma?"

"Fool," Sybilla said.

He started for her, hand upraised.

"Raspberry fool," she said quickly.

"That's better." He lowered his hand slowly. "You're too sharp, Ma, sharp enough to cut yourself. I think we'll have you back in the dining-room with us."

Inga had taken the glasses of frothy pink dessert out of the fridge and lined them up on the table. "Get spoons," she ordered.

Amy fumbled in a drawer, some sort of physical reaction was setting in now, compounded of lack of sleep, too much unaccustomed exercise of her still-weakened hands and, probably, delayed shock.

She brought out three spoons and dropped two. Stooping awkwardly, she gathered them up and placed them on the draining-board. Carefully she selected two more from the drawer, holding them in both hands but still unable to prevent the faint clatter as her shaking hands dropped them beside the glasses.

Aaron watched her with satisfaction. "You can stay here," he told her. "Start washing-up, why don't you? We'll take Lady Muck back to her salon—where I can keep an eye on her."

Inga took the desserts possessively, bunching them together between her hands, the spoons threaded through her fingers, as though flaunting the way normal hands could adapt themselves.

Amy looked away to find Aaron staring at her hands, at the puffy pink sausages that were trying to become fingers again. Vindictiveness flared in his eyes as they met her own.

"*You'll* never be able to do anything like that again," he said.

Chapter 21

Alone in the kitchen, Amy leaned against the sink and closed her eyes. They had marched Sybilla away like a captive, Aaron's animal instinct warning him that, despite her age and her appearance of fragility, she was the source from which danger could come. Amy, on her own, was helpless, particularly in a strange house, still weak, with no knowledge of what Sybilla might have planned. And Sybilla could not tell her now.

Silence closed around her. No sound came from the dining-room; either they were not talking, or else speaking so low that no murmur of voices carried. She had not realized how much moral support Sybilla's presence had given her until now. Now, too, she realized the falsity of that support. How could Sybilla defeat Aaron? She had believed it briefly because she had wanted to—because she had been steeped in the legend of the Invincible Sybilla. With the magnetic presence withdrawn she had to face facts.

But something was different now—Sybilla had had some effect on her own attitude. She opened her eyes and straightened up. She knew now that she was not just going to stand by and let Aaron have it all his own way. She was going to fight.

He had taken all sharp-edged instruments he had

found in his search of the kitchen, but there still must be things left that might serve as weapons. For one thing, she filled the kettle and set it on the gas—boiling water might not be the ultimate deterrent, but it was a start.

Meanwhile, she had been ordered to do the dishes. She turned the hot-water tap on full force, the noise covering the small sounds she made as she eased a drawer open and began her own search.

Aaron hadn't left much. Table knives, forks and spoons, all looking too dull and innocent even to her hopeful eyes. The next drawer held a few wooden spoons, a spatula, egg whisk, dismantled mincing machine, and other cooking tools—nothing remotely lethal.

The sink was nearly full. She turned off the tap and, in the abrupt silence, was conscious of a soft rustling behind her. Had Sybilla managed to get away? She turned swiftly.

"Whatever happens," Sybilla had said. *"Don't speak— don't move."* The words made more sense to her now.

A tall, dark form stood there. Black sweater, slacks, gloves, even blacking on his face. They regarded each other gravely. He was not altogether unfamiliar to her and, gradually, the face beneath the black smears became recognizable.

It was the policeman/gardener who had been keeping watch on the mews and the nursing home.

Except that Sybilla had said the police weren't interested in her, that the police had closed their books on the case and gone away satisfied a long time ago. But he *had* been watching and now he was here, so—if he wasn't the police, who—?

"Good girl," he said, nodding approbation of her silence. "Where's Gran'mère?"

"In the dining-room . . . with them." Her voice was barely a whisper and he nodded approval again. "They're going to keep her with them."

"Much good it will do them." There was a gleam of Sybilla's own amusement in his darkened face. She wondered why she had never noticed the resemblance before except that when she had been looking down from her window on him she had not seen him properly before. She felt a trace of amusement herself, looking at the smudged face. If you could call that seeing him properly . . .

"It looks as though we'll have to introduce ourselves," the man said. "I'm Richard, Richard Sheridan—Sybilla's eldest grandchild, by the son of her first marriage. We're a complicated lot," he added, grinning, "but it sorts itself out as you get to know us better."

"I'm Amy Anderson." She held out her hand automatically, then pulled it back, remembering. He waited and, after a moment, she extended it again.

"We're official, then." He took her hand as gently as Sybilla had done and released it.

"Yes." She felt a smile begin, answering his. "I'm glad you're here. I didn't know—"

"Gran'mère tends to be autocratic," he said. "Has she told you anything at all?"

"Not much," Amy admitted. "I certainly didn't know about you." A thought came to her. "The suitcase—*you* took it."

"Naturally. Gran'mère is also rather possessive. She was most annoyed when they began collecting the valuables."

"I don't blame her," Amy said. "But how did you come to be here? How did you know Aaron would be here tonight?"

"Ah, we've had signals arranged. Every night, Gran'-mère lit every light in the house if all was well. The first night the lights weren't lit, it would mean that the plan had worked. She felt sure that no one occupying a strange house illegally would light any more lights than absolutely necessary—and she was right. As soon as we saw that the house was dark tonight, we went into action."

"But she told me that she—she intended—" Amy found herself stumbling over the statement. It sounded incredible, unreal—yet it had not when Sybilla said it. When Sybilla said it, it had been a simple statement of fact. "She's going to kill Aaron. To avenge Belle."

"Yes." He nodded. "I see she *has* told you some of it."

"But she can't—" Amy protested, as she had protested to Sybilla herself. "They'll put her in prison, or else in a—" Either alternative seemed equally horrible. "She thinks she can get away with it, but—"

"I know," he said. "Gran'mère lived out in the East a long time—perhaps too long. She doesn't seem to realize that she can't mete out her own justice—and have it sit any better with an English court than any of the crimes Aaron has committed. Gran'mère's got a bit too Asiatic in her way of thinking. We've come rather a long way from the 'eye for an eye' philosophy in the West."

"Even so, she couldn't win out over Aaron," Amy said. "She's too—"

"She took on the Japanese army—and won," Richard said. "I can't see a homegrown tearaway defeating her."

"Even if she succeeded, she couldn't get away with it," Amy said. "I know she thinks a psychiatrist—"

"Please—" He held up one hand. "I've *heard* her on the subject!"

"But you're helping her."

"Only up to a point," he said firmly. "Gran'mère may think she wouldn't mind finishing out her days in some expensive loony bin—but *we* mind for her. Furthermore, we think she'd change her mind after the first few months. No matter how much it might resemble a luxury hotel, compared to other places she has known, there *is* a difference. You can walk out of a hotel. So, for her own good, we're not going to let her do it."

"We?" He had used that word before.

"Cousin Sarah has been helping all along." He said

the name as though it should mean something to Amy. "She's back there—" he jerked his head towards the blank wall he had apparently walked through. "You'd better not see her just at the minute. She's looking rather grim."

More blackface, Amy smiled faintly, but there were still too many questions to be answered. "What *exactly* is Sybilla planning? And how can you stop her? She seems awfully determined."

"We don't know exactly what she's planning, but we're going to have a good try at stopping her."

"Are you sure—" she gestured to his blackened face, "you're going about it in the right way?"

"Not *all* Gran'mère's ideas are so bad." He smiled briefly. "We have no objection at all to helping in what she calls her 'psychological warfare.' It's only the final blow we want to keep her from delivering.

"For the rest of it, I see no reason at all why your precious Aaron shouldn't sweat a bit. A lot, in fact. You see—" his face grew cold, hardening into an implacability akin to Sybilla's own—"*we* loved Belle, too."

"He's not *my*—"

"Sorry." He corrected himself almost immediately, with a swift glance at her damaged hands. "Of course, he isn't. I just—"

"It's all right," she forgave him. "It's my—"

"Don't keep saying it's your fault." He sounded angry. "It might have happened to anyone."

"But it happened to *me*."

"And who are you, that you should go through life without a scratch? What guarantee did you ever get that it was sunshine and stardust all the way?"

"No one. None." The deliberate brutality of it startled her into a new awareness. Perhaps that was what he had intended. Other people *had* had hard times, too. Even Sybilla, with all her wealth and position, had had security kicked out from under her, had been forced to live and fight through the hell of a war and a concentration camp. Had survived. More—had had the strength not only to survive, but to have fought for the others imprisoned with her, to have helped them, brought them through the ordeal safely. Was still helping. Sybilla, who had survived so much, and thus was able to pass on the gift that all survivors have: the will to survive.

And, because of that, Sybilla could not now be allowed to take a life. To put herself into a position where justice—blind justice—could condemn her.

"We have to keep behind the scenes," Richard said. "You're out here with her. We don't know what she's got up her sleeve—"

"What *is* behind there?" Amy asked—remembering Sybilla's cool amusement at the thought of being imprisoned in her own house. "There's some kind of passage to the street—another way out, isn't there?"

"Yes . . ." He hesitated. "Do you want to leave? We can take you back to the nursing home, if you like. It isn't fair to put you through any more. Aaron is here—we can go on from there. You can leave any time—"

"No," Amy said. "I *want* to help. What can I do?"

"Good girl." He seemed to relax, as though she had given the right answer, as though it were important to him—personally—that she should. "When you see Sybilla make the first move, try to cut her off. Delay her—and scream at the top of your lungs. By then, it won't make any difference. We can come out in the open and stop her—but it will be up to you to sound the alarm."

"I will," Amy promised. "I don't want to see her locked away, either."

"Good girl," he said again. "Mind you," he added ruefully, "perhaps she ought to be. I don't suppose her immediate loved ones are in the best position to judge the situation. But even we have to admit that we feel towards her right now rather as Wellington is said to have felt towards his troops."

She found herself smiling again. She had read enough English history to recognize the quotation he referred to. "You mean—"

"That's right." He paraphrased cheerfully. "I don't know whether she scares the enemy but, by God, she scares *us*!"

She heard the unfamilar sound of her own laughter with astonishment. Not loud—thank heaven—but genuine. How long had it been since she had been able to laugh? She looked at him with gratitude. "Richard—"

Footsteps were coming down the hall. Richard ducked back against the wall, out of sight to anyone who might come through the doorway. His gesture for silence was superfluous—she had forgotten what she wanted to tell him.

"Aaron says—" George stepped through the doorway— "where's the—"

The black-gloved hand clamped down over his mouth, he was caught and lifted backwards and sideways. A portion of the wall swung inwards and they both melted into the woodwork.

"You didn't—" a disembodied voice hung in the kitchen, instructing Amy—"see a thing."

Chapter 22

Amy turned back to the sink and ran cold water into it, testing cautiously with a fingertip until it reached a temperature she could bear. There had been a dish rack under the sink; she got it out and set it on the draining-board. She stood looking at the steaming water for a moment, then plunged her hands into it and groped for the slippery dishes. It was another minor triumph when she grasped one, wiped it round with the dishcloth and placed it safely in the rack.

It was so silent in the kitchen that she could hear the drops of water falling from the dish on to the draining-board, and then the kettle began to hiss steam. For a curiously dreamlike moment, as she crossed to turn off the gas under the boiling kettle, it seemed domestic and peaceful. As though she were in a haven, rather than trapped in some kind of maze with an enemy intent on killing her.

Still she moved dreamily, almost dissociated from what she was doing. Perhaps the sudden realization that she was not alone, that she had allies—seen and unseen —had sent her into a state of shock. Or brought her out of one. For the first time in months, she was aware that she had begun to function again on some previously buried level. Automatically, she continued with her chore, waiting for the next move in the game. But whose game would it be: Aaron's or Sybilla's?

There was only the faintest of sounds behind her, but she whirled about, expecting to see that Richard had come back. Aaron stood in the doorway, watching her.

"Where's George?" he demanded.

"I don't know." She forced herself to turn away, leaving her back exposed to him. "I haven't seen him."

"He came down here." She heard Aaron move into the room, his footsteps light as a cat's on the polished linoleum.

"Look at me when I'm talking to you." His hand on her shoulder spun her round to face him again. "George *came* down here. Where is he?"

"I haven't seen him," she repeated. Her eyes widened as, behind him, Sybilla appeared noiselessly in the doorway and began advancing silently towards him. Was she about to make her move?

"What the—?" He whirled around and seemed almost relieved to find it was only Sybilla. "What are you doing here? I told you to stay in the other room."

Sybilla shrugged a shoulder. It was clear that that was as much of an answer as he was going to get.

"Where's Inga?" He transferred his truculence. "I told that stupid cow to watch you."

Sybilla lifted her other shoulder. Her air of command was more apparent now. It would be a reckless au pair girl who tried to stop her from doing anything she wanted to do.

Amy suddenly wondered if, during her years in the Orient, Sybilla had learned karate. If so, then she would need no weapon at all to dispose of Aaron. A sudden pounce, a blow or two on the right spot—and that would be that. There would be no time to scream a warning, no time to stop her. Instinctively, she knew that Sybilla could move faster than she could. Furthermore, Sybilla knew exactly what she was going to do—and had divulged her plan to no one else.

It was, of course, the classic formula for success. But it was exceedingly hard on one's allies.

"George *came* down here." Aaron kept worrying the thought. "Where is he?"

"Where's your suitcase full of silver?" Sybilla asked.

"You think—? No. No," Aaron denied.

"No?" Her smile was without humour.

"You're trying to turn us against each other. I'm on to your game. George is still here—he's *got* to be."

"Where?" Sybilla's glance roamed around the kitchen, pointedly lingering in every empty corner.

"He's here." Aaron's gaze followed her own, probing, insistent. "He's *got* to be."

"Why don't you call him?" Sybilla taunted, lazily amused. "Are you afraid he won't answer?"

"George!" Giving her a baleful glare, Aaron responded to the challenge. "GEORGE!"

His voice echoed in the silence. Then, abruptly, there were hurrying footsteps coming down the hall.

"There—" Aaron could not hide the relief in his voice. "You see—" He broke off abruptly.

"What is?" It was Inga who entered the room. "Why you shout George? He is here with you." She looked around the room slowly, disbelievingly.

"He is here with you," she repeated, against the evidence of her eyes.

"Does it look like he is, you stupid cow?"

"He *come* out here."

"Sure, he did. But he's not here now, is he?" Aaron moved forward, his hand slightly swung out, as though he might be going to strike her again, to work off some of his bad temper on her.

"Where he go?" Inga drew herself up, pulling the blonde mink closely about her, the tilt of her head an imitation of Sybilla's.

"Watch these two," Aaron ordered. "I'm going to take a look around and find out."

Inga moved in nervous protest as he left the room. He halted in the doorway to turn and glare at her. "Do as I say!"

Irresolute, Inga moved back, watching him go. There was an uneasy shadow on her face, as though she sensed how close he had come to violence.

Sybilla smiled at Amy and moved across the room. Instantly, Inga whirled on her.

"Where you go?"

"I want a glass of water." Sybilla paused and looked at Inga thoughtfully. "Is that all right? Or—" authority rippled beneath her voice—"would you like to get it for me?"

"No." Inga stood back, allowing Sybilla access to the sink. She watched nervously as Sybilla filled a glass and drank slowly. Overhead, they could hear Aaron thumping through the rooms again, following his progress as he searched the same corners he had searched for the suitcase—not many of them big enough to have possibly accommodated George.

"We go other room," Inga decided. She looked around the kitchen with distaste, obviously reminded of her recent lowly status by it. She had done too much work here, she wished to be in a setting more fitting to a fine lady in a mink.

"As you wish." Placidly, Sybilla led the way to the living-room, Amy followed immediately behind her. Inga brought up the rear, looking unhappy and as though she were vaguely aware that the situation was getting out of hand—out of her hands. She looked up as they passed the foot of the stairs, but only a furious muttering from above gave any indication of Aaron's presence. It did not seem to be enough to satisfy Inga.

Amy had not seen the living-room properly before; now that it had been restored to order, she seemed to know it. She hesitated in the doorway, trying to identify the nightmarish familiarity.

"Come in and sit down," Sybilla said crisply. "Don't stand there looking as though you'd seen a ghost."

And that, of course, was it. This was the ghost of a room she had known. It was the mirror image of the drawing-room in the big Victorian flat that had belonged to Sybil's family. The flat that was now destroyed—utterly and completely—beyond reconstruction.

Yet, this room lived on. Not quite the same. As the house was not the same. But the spirit was so closely akin that it conveyed the same sort of feeling, the same sense of identity.

It was a much smaller room, the furnishings scaled down to size. The miniatures on the walls were different miniatures, but in the same places. The arrangement of the furniture was the same.

She was giddy with the sudden sense of unreality, of being dislocated in time. She had the feeling that Ginny should be sitting in the chair where Inga slumped, that Belle would come through the door, laughing, at any moment.

But—she tried to pull herself together—perhaps this was just some sort of standard English décor, repeated over and over in endless homes. She might be putting too much of an interpretation on something that was simply an accident of design.

Then she looked at Sybilla's face and knew that this was deliberate. It had been carefully planned, as everything Sybilla had arranged so far had been carefully planned.

"Come and sit down," Sybilla said again. She had seated herself on the sofa and now she patted the cushion beside her. "Come over here and sit down."

Slowly, Amy crossed to the sofa, so like the one which had nearly been her funeral pyre. She did not want to sit on it, but a curiously dreamlike state had taken over, coupled with the knowledge that everything was out of her hands—her useless hands—and in Sybilla's capable ones. Everything was moving forward according to some preconceived plan.

Sybilla gave her a radiant smile of approval as she sat down. Amy smiled back wanly.

They heard Aaron at the head of the stairs, he seemed to be muttering to himself, or perhaps to a George he thought might be hiding nearby.

Sybilla stretched out her hand and touched the base of the lamp on the table behind the sofa. Amy was not surprised when the lights were immediately extinguished.

"The light—" Inga began.

"Then go and get the candles from the other room," Sybilla directed.

Outside, they heard Aaron stumble, catch himself, and curse. "Bring a light, you cow!" he shouted.

"I do not like this," Inga complained. As their eyes grew accustomed once again to darkness, they could discern the darker shadow of her passage as she went across the hallway to retrieve the lighted candles.

"One's taste improves as one grows older," Sybilla said, as though she had seen Amy's wince at Aaron's shout. "You'll see." Almost as a non-sequitur, she added, "My grandson likes you."

"Your taste wasn't so good," Amy fired a hasty shot in her own defence, "when you hired Inga."

"On the contrary," Sybilla said. "Inga was precisely what I was looking for. She is sly, lazy, amoral, and completely untrustworthy. She'd betray her own parents, far less an employer, if she thought it would gain her a moment's favour with anything in trousers. You have no idea of the number of interviews I conducted before I found her.

"In fact—" the smile was audible in Sybilla's voice —"I'm sure that some of the good ladies at the employment agencies will be willing to testify that I was quite mad to hire her when I had refused so many excellent

applicants for the position I had in mind. It's as well—"
the amusement in her voice deepened—"that they didn't
realize exactly what that position *was*. Inga has filled it to
perfection."

Voices were raised in the hall outside, but not audibly
enough to distinguish words. There was a brightness near
the doorway which suggested Inga was on her way with
the dining-room candles.

The voices grew louder—notably Aaron's, rising above
a Scandinavian whine of protest. Then, sharp and violent
as a pistol shot, the crack of flesh against flesh—after
which, abrupt utter silence.

The room warmed and brightened into life as Aaron
entered, carrying a lighted candelabrum. In the light and
shadow effect of the flames his face was a flickering mask,
given more movement by the play of candlelight than was
to be found in his rigidly set muscles. He seemed to be
holding himself carefully in check.

"All alone?" Sybilla's voice arched like her eyebrows
in well-modulated surprise. "You haven't found your friend?"
She ignored Inga, who sidled through the doorway behind
him and slumped into the nearest chair, huddled in her
mink, one hand nursing her cheek.

"He's here somewhere." Aaron set the candelabrum
down on the coffee-table between the sofa and the over-
stuffed chairs, his expression momentarily bemused, as
though uneasy memories were stirring in his consciousness.

"I suppose *you* still have the key to the front door?"
Sybilla inquired languidly.

"That's right, *I* have." Aaron dived into a pocket,
producing the key immediately.

"I suppose it's the right key?"

"Why wouldn't it be?" The doubt had never occurred
to him, they watched him struggle with it now. "I locked
the door and put the key in my pocket myself."

"Of course," Sybilla murmured, appearing to lose interest.

"That's right." Aaron seemed to be trying to convince himself. "Right in my pocket. Nobody could get it without me knowing." He glared at her as though she had challenged this statement. "Nobody."

Sybilla shrugged.

"Right," he said. "I'll prove it to you. Come out here—" He started for the front door. "*Come* on."

Indifferently, taking up the candelabrum, Sybilla moved to follow him. Not sure whether the command included her, Amy went too. Even Inga got up and drifted slowly in their wake, remaining in the shadows by the doorway.

"See—" Aaron stabbed the key at the lock, inserting it, turning it. "See—" He pulled at the door. Nothing happened.

"See—" he repeated again, disbelieving as the door refused to budge. "See—" Desperately, he twisted the key backwards and forwards, trying the door after each turn. They could hear the click of tumblers, but nothing happened. The door remained obdurate.

"Is locked," Inga voiced the obvious. "Is wrong key."

"You bloody bitch!" Aaron whirled, a bright gleam flashed in the darkness, then Inga gasped as the heavy chunk of metal struck her forehead and dropped to the floor. "*You* gave it to me. I got *in* with it. Don't tell *me* it's the wrong key."

One hand to her forehead, Inga dipped to the floor and retrieved the key. Moving only slightly forward to get a better light on it, she frowned at the object in her hand. "*Is* right key," she agreed sulkily. "I remember."

"Then why doesn't it work?" Aaron was almost screaming in rage and frustration. "Why won't it open the door?"

Inga gave a shrug, much like Sybilla's. Her face was shuttered, closed against him, against them all. A small blob of blood welled at the point on her temple where the key had struck. She brushed her forehead with the back of her hand, then stared incredulously at the smear of blood on it. She glanced across at Aaron and her eyes glittered dangerously.

He didn't notice. He had turned his attention to Sybilla. "Come on, Ma," he said. "Where's the right key?"

"That looks like the right key to me." Sybilla smiled blandly. "If it isn't, I can only suggest you ask your cohort that question—*if* you ever find him again." She turned and swept back into the living-room, leaving them abruptly in darkness as the candelabrum went with her.

The darkness turned the hallway into a tunnel, with Aaron still standing at the farther end. Amy moved quickly to follow the receding brightness. Inga stood at the foot of the stairs, brooding, seemingly unaware of them all.

Amy was just at the threshold when she heard Aaron's hoarse scream. Looking back, she could distinguish the paleness of his hand against the blackness. It was pointing upwards and beyond her. She turned, looking upward to the landing of the stairs and just barely choked back a cry of her own.

Belle!

Belle was hovering there.

Chapter 23

Belle, a pale yellow-green glow emanating from her, dressed as she had been on that last day. Over those clothes she seemed to be wearing some sort of cloak, above which her neck and face floated, beneath which her shoulders were grotesquely, obscenely twisted.

Amy drew a deep breath, unsteady but silent. Aaron's cry had not drawn Sybilla back into the hallway. Why should it? She knew what was out here. There were faint sounds of movement in the living-room. Sybilla, preparing for whatever was to come next.

Amy tried to move, but found herself weak, trembling with shock. Intellectually, she knew what must be happening. "*Sarah,*" Richard had said, "*is looking a bit grim at the moment.*" "*The house belonged to a famous stage designer,*" little Nurse Jellicoe had said. "*He used to give fabulous entertainments there.*"

Little Nurse Jellicoe—no wonder it had hurt to look at her sometimes. It had not been because of the shining radiance with which she could view an untarnished life stretching out before her. It had been the unacknowledged resemblance she bore to Belle, stronger at some moments than at others, from which Amy had shrunk. Sarah Jellicoe, a nurse, after all, and not a policewoman. Keeping her hair tucked up under the nurse's cap, when

Belle's had always flowed free, had helped to disguise the likeness. Sarah, who must be one of Belle's "middle cousins" and Sybilla's granddaughter through the daughter of her second marriage. Now that one knew, the family resemblance was unmistakable.

Amy found she was regaining control. Her breathing had steadied, but her legs would not yet move, would not carry her into the living-room.

On the landing, still bathed in that eerie glow, "Belle" had been staring accusingly at Aaron, who was backed against the front door uttering strangled croaks of protest. Now she half turned her back to them, mouth open in a silent scream, her hands floated upwards as though to drop her cloak and reveal those poor mangled shoulders.

"No!" Aaron whirled, clawing at the door for escape. It remained obdurate and, slowly, half-crouched, ready to fight what could not be fought, he swung back again.

Belle vanished even as he looked up at her. One second she was there, the next second the landing was empty.

There was a rush of footsteps and Amy felt herself flung aside as Aaron darted down the hallway and into the living-room. The words he began shouting at Sybilla were loud, but incomprehensible. He had reverted to some dialect Amy could not interpret, and she suspected that she had never heard some of the words before anyway.

Amy entered the living-room slowly. Behind her, she heard Inga give a faint sigh, and the whisper of hands stroking fur as though to gain comfort from it, then a stirring as Inga followed her into the room.

Sybilla was sitting on the sofa, leaning back, completely relaxed, regarding Aaron with the same detached disgust with which she might have viewed some particularly revolting specimen on a microscope slide.

"*You* saw it!" he shouted at Amy, as she entered. "*You* saw it!" he accused Inga.

Inga drew herself up, clutching the mink around her. "I see nothing," she repudiated coldly.

"Don't give me that—" He advanced on her menacingly. "*You* saw it. You saw it before—the time you screamed. That was why you screamed. That was what you saw."

"No!" Inga set her jaw mulishly. "I never see nothing. Nothing there."

"*You* saw it!" He turned on Amy.

"Saw what?" She would make him say it, admit it.

"Her—your friend. The one who— The one you called Belle."

"I've seen Belle every day since she died," Amy admitted truthfully. "I think I shall see her every day for the rest of my life."

Sybilla stirred slightly. The movement drew Aaron's attention.

"What about you, Ma? You're being awfully quiet— for you. Do you know what we're talking about? Do you, Ma?"

"Yes," Sybilla said. "I do."

"You do?" He faced her uncertainly. She had not been in the hall to see. "Then maybe you can explain what this is all about. What's that—that *thing* doing haunting *your* house?"

"Why shouldn't she be here?" Sybilla met his eyes with a cold inscrutable gaze. "This is her home."

"Don't hand me anything funny, Ma—I'm not in the mood."

"You destroyed her home. There's nothing left of the family flat. You never went back to see what you had done. It was completely burnt out—gutted."

Amy shuddered.

"Belle—her spirit—could not stay there. And so, she came here—to me. Where she belonged."

"She did?" Aaron had begun backing away slowly. "Why was that? What was she to you, Ma? Who are you?"

"She was my granddaughter," Sybilla said. "My youngest granddaughter."

"Look, M— Look, lady—" Aaron seemed to be having trouble breathing. "This is all crazy—*you're* crazy. She's dead. The dead don't come back—" He closed his eyes briefly, as though the vision of Belle had presented itself to him again. "It isn't true. Why should she come back?"

"She is here—" Sybilla's voice was as chill and remote as the look in her eyes—"because she knew you'd be coming. She's been waiting for you to arrive. We've both been waiting for you."

"What do you want?" Suddenly, he believed it, believed anything. "What do you *want*?"

Sybilla smiled.

"You're crazy," Aaron gasped. "You're raving mad!"

"You killed my granddaughter," Sybilla said. "I intend to see that you never kill anyone else."

Aaron whirled abruptly and hurled himself at the nearest window, clawing at the iron nails he had driven into it earlier. Outside, a faint rim of grey outlined the other houses along the mews and the flood lights atop the nursing home no longer seemed so blindingly bright. It would soon be dawn.

In the corner, Inga's brooding eyes glittered; she stared at Aaron as though measuring the narrowness of what might have been her own escape. She pulled the mink closer, but seemed to find no comfort in it.

Aaron was battering at the window glass itself now, but the glass was unbreakable. Defeated, he turned back to face into the room, his hands bleeding from the unavailing struggle.

"She's crazy." Aaron appealed, first to Inga, then to Amy. "She can't get away with it."

"On the contrary," Sybilla said. "You are already dead.

The police ascertained that to their own satisfaction and closed their case records. You no longer exist. Who can kill a dead man?"

She hadn't moved, but he retreated before her. "She doesn't mean it," he said to Amy. "She can't."

Amy stared at him dispassionately. She had been afraid of him for what seemed so long. She had been hypnotized by the certain knowledge of his revenge, awaiting her fate with a passivity that was now beginning to astonish her.

As he looked from Sybilla to Inga to Amy, his whole face seemed to blur, as his lips were blurred by the partially erased make-up. Faced with a genuinely dangerous adversary, a hatred more implacable than his own, his façade was crumbling.

He was nothing but a bully. Just a— What was it Richard had said? *A home-grown tearaway.* Without a victim he could terrorize, without his cohorts to back him up, to pose before, he was nothing.

"All right." He dropped to a crouch again. "All right. Now I know. You're not so smart, M—lady. You shouldn't have warned me. Now I can take care of whatever you're going to do—"

A swift movement for his trouser pocket, a click, and a long thin stiletto glittered in his hand. "Come on," he snarled. "Come on and try something."

Inga stared at the tip of the glittering knife as though mesmerized. She raised a hand to touch the drying rivulet of blood on her forehead, then lowered the hand quickly and defensively to cover her throat. Her knowledge of the English language might be far from perfect, but it was obvious that a few salient messages were beginning to get through.

Sybilla regarded Aaron coldly. "What do you imagine you're doing?"

"I'll tell you what I'm doing, M—lady." Aaron glared

at her wildly. "I'm defending myself. You're not going to get *me*. Come on—" He waved the knife. "Come on and try. I can take care of myself. No old hag is going to get *Aaron*. Better men than you have tried—*men*. And I'm still around. I'll cut up anyone who comes near me."

"I see." Sybilla leaned back against the cushions. "You believe violence is the answer to everything, don't you? You think a knife can save you?"

"I *know* it can, lady. It won't be the first time. So, come on. I'm ready for you."

"On the contrary." Sybilla smiled. "You're too late. You've already eaten it."

Chapter 24

Aaron turned grey. A thin film of perspiration gave an unhealthy sheen to his face in the candlelight. "What do you mean?"

But he knew. Fascinated, Amy watched the tip of the knife reflecting the light as it danced like a firefly in the darkness with the trembling of Aaron's hand.

"WHAT DO YOU MEAN?" This time, he screamed it, his voice cracking at the end.

"*When you see her make her move,*" Richard had said, "*scream and we'll come.*" But Sybilla had long since made her move, silently and unseen. It was all over. Had she known Sarah and Richard were planning to foil her if they could? More than likely she had. That was why she had diverted them with theatrical games, side-tracking their attention, lulling their suspicions. Keeping them safely out of the way, like children sent to play "Dressing-up" in the attic, out from under Grannie's feet, while she got on with the real business of the day.

"I can do you, you old bitch, you know." Aaron crept closer, the knife weaving in front of him. "I can do all three of you and nobody can stop me—nobody will ever know."

"Do you think so?" Sybilla arched an eyebrow incredulously. "Are you sure you're feeling strong enough to?"

"What—?" Aaron blinked. Almost of its own volition, his arm began to drop as though the knife were growing too heavy to hold. "You didn't." He forced his arm up again. "You wouldn't dare. You don't do things like that. Not your sort."

"My sort?" Sybilla looked as though she might laugh. "What does *your* sort know about *my* sort?"

"She is devil," Inga volunteered. "Always complain . . . always faulting . . ." A worried frown had been growing on her face. "Devil—she do *any* thing!" Inga summarized, with conviction. One hand stayed at her throat, the other crept to her stomach, slipping beneath the mink, which seemed to have lost much of its power to reassure her.

"It leaves no trace," Sybilla said. "If it came down to it, it would be my word against yours—and I believe I have a better reputation."

"Oh, you do, do you?" Aaron was still struggling between disbelief and terror. "And what—?"

"Isn't that your friend?" Sybilla looked past him, indicating the window.

"What—?" Aaron whirled round.

Against the pale grey light outside, they could see George, standing some distance from the front door, surveying the house with a puzzled frown, as though wondering what had happened and how he had suddenly found himself on the outside looking in.

"Come back, you!" Aaron hurled himself towards the window, shouting. "Come back here!" He hammered on the window pane and gesticulated wildly.

George moved farther back, his face hardened, meeting Aaron's fury with a fury of his own. He raised a fist and shook it at Aaron.

Amy realized that George had not seen the assailant who had taken him from behind. Perhaps he had been unconscious for a while. He could have no idea that there

was anyone else in the house—and the suitcase full of
valuables had disappeared before he had been attacked.
He could only believe that Aaron had struck him down
and hurled him out of the house in order not to have to
split the loot with him. No wonder his face was growing
mottled with rage, the light of revenge beginning to blaze
in his eyes.

"What's the matter with you? You're crazy!" Aaron
shouted, unheard through the thick glass.

Still shaking his fist, George backed until his features
had dissolved into the darkness, leaving his face a pale
moon bobbing down the mews. Then, apparently feeling
himself safe from pursuit, he turned his back, striding
determinedly towards the telephone kiosk at the entrance
to the mews.

Inga shifted restlessly and the movement seemed to
explode in Aaron's ears. He whirled about to face the
room, knife at the ready.

"Don't any of you move," he commanded. "You're
not going to jump *me*."

"There won't be any need for that," Sybilla said calmly.
Less than half her attention seemed centred on Aaron, the
rest was intent upon the scene at the far end of the mews,
where George had entered the telephone kiosk and could
be clearly seen inside the brightly lit box.

"What do you mean?" Aaron glared at her savagely.
"You're trying to break me down, aren't you, lady? You
think you can scare me to death. You think I'm going to
fall apart any minute."

"Oh no," Sybilla countered. "It won't be that quick.
It will take a long time—weeks, months, possibly years. I
wanted you to have a long time to know what's happening
to you. Much longer than my granddaughter had."

Amy turned her eyes from Aaron's face. The growing
shock registered there was almost too painful to watch,
even knowing what he had done, even having hated him

for so long. She looked beyond him, out of the window, focusing on the telephone kiosk.

George was dialling, she watched him. His arm moved in three long strokes, the same number each time: 9-9-9. Then he hunched forward over the mouthpiece, speaking briefly but forcefully. When he stopped speaking, he broke off the connection, swung open the door and stepped out of the kiosk. He cocked his head, as though listening for the sound of oncoming police cars, raised his hand in a derisory two-fingered gesture aimed down the mews, then melted rapidly away into the grey dawn, heading for the West End where he could lose himself amongst the early morning traffic.

So help was on the way. The police would have to investigate an anonymous tip-off like that. Somehow, she was sure that George had sounded sufficiently author-itative to activate the emergency services immediately. Amy wanted to relax now, to be able to feel that it was all over, but she could not. She had already seen what Aaron could do in the space of just a few seconds when he found himself cornered.

"No . . ." He was speaking in a reflective murmur, almost to himself now. "Let me think this through. You're trying to scare me . . . confuse me . . . until it's too late. So there's got to be a reason . . ."

Amy watched Sybilla's face tighten and knew that Aaron was striking close to home. Sybilla, too, had been observing George's actions.

"Got to be a reason . . ." Aaron was still battling his way through to some sort of understanding. "What?" He hurled the question at Sybilla, as though the suddenness might cut through her guard and force her to blurt out an answer. The technique had probably worked quite well in his dealings with people like Zlot and George.

But he could not dominate Sybilla, nor surprise her into anything she did not intend to reveal. With a faint smile on her lips, she looked through Aaron as though he had ceased to exist.

"Confuse me . . . keep me from thinking . . . thinking . . . what? Thinking about *you*, maybe, and this house. This house . . ."

Sybilla's eyes were alert.

"Such a nice neat little house. A place for everything and everything in its place, isn't that right? Isn't it?" He lunged suddenly, plunging the knife into the arm of the sofa, drawing it along sharply, the stuffing spilling out in its wake.

Sybilla didn't move, the knife had missed her by about six inches. He had not intended to hit her, but he needed to destroy, to ruin something. Amy drew a deep breath, but a minuscule movement of Sybilla's hand checked her incipient scream.

Inga, too, had drawn in her breath sharply. Now she glanced across at Sybilla, studying her thoughtfully before her eyes moved to look at Aaron warily. Her shoulders moved restlessly under the mink, as though the weight of the coat were becoming a burden to her.

"A place for everything . . . *everything*." His eyes brightened. "You have everything, haven't you? From a silver teapot to a dose of poison. And, if you've got poison, then you've got an antidote around here somewhere, haven't you?" He was talking more rapidly, convincing himself, his eyes flicking from Sybilla to the doorway as he spoke.

"A place for everything . . . The place for that would be the medicine cabinet in the bathroom, wouldn't it?" His face was feverish, his eyes glittered. "That's right," he answered his own question. "There'll be an antidote in the medicine cabinet." He half turned towards Inga.

"Get it!" he ordered.

Inga edged forward slowly, moving with extreme care, as though mentally working out a complicated translation, the thread of which might be broken by any sudden movement.

"Hurry up!"

Inga was on her feet, frowning. "How I know which is?"

"You know what's usually in the medicine cabinet, don't you? Look for any bottles you don't recognize. If there's more than one, bring them all down." He gestured with his knife. "Move!"

While waiting for Inga to return, he patrolled the room in a sideways crab crawl, keeping his eyes fixed on Sybilla. She appeared to have abdicated, mentally removing herself to some distant spot, sitting so motionless she might have turned to stone.

Only the faint rise and fall of Sybilla's breathing, scarcely rippling the brocade jacket, reassured Amy. Fortunately, Aaron seemed to have forgotten her. All his animosity was centred on Sybilla in a concentrated blaze of fear and fury that threatened to break its bounds at any moment and send him hurtling towards her throat with his knife.

The sound of Inga's returning footsteps halted him in his tracks. He moved quickly to the doorway, but Inga appeared to be in no hurry. Almost visibly, his hackles rose as he waited, not quite daring to turn his back on Sybilla, nor leave her unguarded long enough to stray out into the hall. He had learned; he would not underestimate her again.

There was a long hesitation outside the door. Inga obviously wasn't happy about returning, but knew there was no alternative. If she didn't return, Aaron would go and hunt her down.

"Come on! Come on!"

Slowly she entered, clutching a small vial with both hands. "Is only this," she said.

"Well, give it to me." Aaron snatched it from her. "Is

this the right one?" He darted over to wave it in front of Sybilla's face. "Answer me, is it?"

Sybilla moved her head back slightly, the only indication she gave of being aware he was there. She could not help glancing at the bottle and something flickered in her eyes, alerting him.

"It is!" he cried triumphantly. "It's the antidote!" He wrenched the cap off and raised the bottle to his lips. Then he hesitated, brought the bottle up to eye level, stared at it incredulously and lowered it again.

"What *is* this?" He turned on Inga furiously. "What did you bring this for? It's empty."

"Was not enough for two." Inga shrugged, seeming perplexed at his surprise. "I am eat what you eat. I am not wish to die.

"*I* drink."

Chapter 25

Sybilla laughed aloud.

"Bitch!" His clown-face contorted, he hurled the empty bottle away and leaped for Inga, slashing out with his knife.

Inga screamed and jumped back, raising her arm to protect her throat. There was a painful tearing sound as the blade ripped through fur and hide, seeking flesh.

Sybilla rose swiftly, reaching for the candelabrum. The candles flared and died as she swept it up, leaving little slipstreams of smoke to mark their rapid progress towards the back of Aaron's head. The room was filled with a pale grey light—it was dawn outside.

Struggling with Inga, Aaron moved suddenly just as the candelabrum was descending. It glanced harmlessly off his shoulder, reminding him of the enemy he had momentarily forgotten. He whirled and advanced upon Sybilla. This time there was no doubt that he intended to use the knife. Inga screamed again.

She had been heard the first time. Richard rushed into the room, halting just inside the doorway to appraise the situation.

Moving swiftly to escape Aaron's murderous fury, Sybilla trod on the bottle he had flung away and her foot twisted under her, plummeting her to the carpet. Aaron closed in quickly, raising the knife above her. Sybilla turned to meet the blade, watching her chance to gain any advantage.

Almost unnoticed, Richard rushed forward. Sarah appeared in the doorway he had vacated, still glowing a phosphorescent green, looking worse in the pale grey light than she had in the complete blackness of the hall.

Inga saw her and screamed again, this time with such terror that Aaron's hand was temporarily stayed. Sybilla rolled away as he turned to see the reason for Inga's screams. He muttered a curse at the apparition and brought his attention back to Sybilla, but she was not where he had last seen her. Before he could locate her again, Richard was upon him.

Amy moved, skirting the edges of the room, to help Sybilla to her feet. Inga had subsided into whimpering sobs interspersed with incoherent mutterings in her own language as the battle raged around her and the apparition in the doorway refused to disappear. Obviously feeling that some sort of retribution was about to be visited upon her, Inga slithered out of the mink coat as though disposing of the evidence and moved away from it, dissociating herself from it.

Aaron broke free of Richard's grasp and backed, gaining distance and space in which to use his knife. Richard had only his bare hands.

Sybilla was still getting her breath back, but she gestured imperiously towards the candelabrum she had dropped. Amy looked at it hopelessly, knowing that her aching hands could never grasp it firmly enough to deliver a telling blow. She was swept by rage at her helplessness. Desperately, she looked around.

Aaron was crouching once more, knife at the ready, obviously hoping Richard would charge. But Richard was wary, knowing that the rules he respected were weaknesses in a battle with someone who acknowledged no rules. Richard waited for Aaron to take the initiative.

There wasn't long to wait. Aaron lurched forward suddenly, knife poised for the deadly upward thrust that would slide under the defensive rib cage and penetrate heart or lungs.

Sybilla moaned faintly. Was she to lose another grandchild to this madman? And, this one she had brought into the danger zone herself.

Amy stooped and caught up the discarded mink. In the same moment, she shook out the folds, stepped forward and swirled the coat down over Aaron's head.

The knife connected harmlessly with satin lining and hide, caught, and was entangled. Richard closed in to knock out Aaron and disarm him.

A flashing blue light began to illumine the room spasmodically, like flashes of summer lightning. Amy looked outside, to see the dark car moving slowly down the mews.

"Quickly," Sybilla said. "Out of sight, you two. We'll take care of this now. And remember—you were never here." She stepped forward to the window, signalling urgently, as Richard and Sarah drifted back into the front hall. Unless one knew what to listen for, the faintest click of a panel closing would have been inaudible.

"Ja, we fix," Inga seconded determinedly. She sat down abruptly and none-too-gently on Aaron's head, motioning Amy to sit on his legs. Inga, too, was a survivor. More than a survivor—with her eye for the winning side and ability to about-face quickly, Inga was one of life's winners.

Two figures in dark blue were at the front door now. They seemed to be fumbling with something at the side, but the bell, of course, didn't ring.

"Over here!" Sybilla rapped on the window pane sharply. "The door won't open." She sagged against the window frame, looking frail and exhausted.

"We've been locked in," she told them. "You'll have to break the window."

*   *   *

Late that afternoon, Inga served tea, looking neat and
tidy in a black dress with frilly white apron, her attitude
polite and demure, if not actually respectful. An improbable
Inga, but the men balancing their tea things as they made
notes didn't know that.

Amy had met one of the men before, when she and
Ginny had been taken to his office by Belle—it seemed so
long ago now. Everything seemed so very distant, as
though she had awakened from a long nightmare.

Upstairs, in the guestroom, she had slept for hours—
without the aid of any pills. Upon awakening, she had
found her needlework frame standing beside a chair in
front of the window, her slippers by the bed, her clothes
in the closet. Sarah had been very busy while she slept.

Sarah, trim in her nurse's uniform again, but without
the misleading cap, sat beside her on the sofa. From
outside in the mews, came the sound of hedge clippers as
Richard began working out his week's notice at the nursing home.

Sybilla poured second cups, once more serene and
ageless, secure in her own setting, looking as though no
trouble or tragedy had ever brushed close to her, let alone
involved her.

Inga set down a fresh jug of milk and stepped back. "I
wish to go home," she announced. It was not the first time
today she had said so. "I am not stay here."

"Perhaps that *would* be best." Sybilla looked to her
authoritative friends for confirmation. "The poor child *has*
had a frightful time."

As though on cue, Inga drooped appealingly. Amy
raised her cup to her lips and refused to meet Sarah's
eyes. Sybilla had obviously had a very busy morning.

"Surely," Sybilla continued smoothly, "she could be
allowed to go. Would it not be enough if she left a deposition behind for the trial?"

Once again, Amy admired Sybilla's strategy. A written deposition would be ideal. Just a flat statement of "fact" on a piece of unchanging paper—with no Inga in person to be confused by cross-questioning and diverted along dangerous byways.

"Oh, it shouldn't come to that," the elder man said reassuringiy. "A trial, I mean. The fellow's obviously unfit to plead. He's been babbling about ghosts, things disappearing—all sorts of rot. Even claims you've poisoned him with something untraceable."

"Really?" Sybilla smiled faintly. "But I've always understood that there's no such thing as an untraceable poison. It doesn't exist."

"Precisely," the man said. "Apart from which, the prison doctors have given him a thorough examination. He's right as rain—except mentally. Oh, yes, it's Broadmoor for that one, all right. And they're not so keen on letting psychopathic murderers out again these days—not after the last few little mishaps when they've tried it. Good behaviour isn't going to fool them quite so much any more. No, Broadmoor is a lot more final than a prison sentence these days."

"Yes." Sybilla smiled more widely. "So I understand."

Amy glanced at her quickly, then glanced away, the undercurrent in Sybilla's tone echoing in her mind. Aaron—locked away in an asylum instead of a prison, which would be even worse for him. In a place where he would not be able to communicate satisfactorily with the other inmates—because they were mad and he was sane. But, the more he tried to convince anyone of the truth of his story, the more insane he would sound. Aaron—proved mad for telling the truth.

At no point, Amy recalled now, had Sybilla actually declared she intended to kill Aaron. The word she had used was "destroy." And Aaron, in Broadmoor, still convinced that he was dying a slow death from poison, was as surely destroyed as though he were already dead. But it was a long, endlessly nightmarish, living death he had been condemned to.

It was hideously cruel. It was barbaric. It was—*Asiatic*.

Amy moved forward, setting down her cup, opening her mouth to speak out.

"More tea?" Sybilla turned to her swiftly, meeting her eyes warningly. Amy looked into the blue depths of Sybilla's eyes and met Belle there. Belle, who had died so horribly, to whom Aaron had shown no mercy.

Amy lowered her eyes, to her hands, to the fingers which would, eventually, come back to normal—no thanks to Aaron. Inevitably, she thought of Ginny.

Aaron *was* mad, but not—until now—certifiably so. Amy flexed her fingers reflectively and smiled across at Sybilla.

"Just half a cup," she murmured. "Thank you."

"I think that's all." Sybilla's guests rose to their feet. "We can come back to you if we need anything more."

"Of course," Sybilla agreed.

"Yes—" the man looked thoughtfully from Sybilla to Amy's hands, to Inga, so wan and unhappy—"he's even claiming some strong-arm thug got rid of his partner and overcame him."

"They quarrelled—" Sybilla shook her head sadly— "and his accomplice walked out. After that, he got worse and worse—Thank heaven the other one was furious enough to telephone the police with his anonymous tip—"

"Oh, I don't know," the man said. "You seemed to have the situation well in hand when the police arrived. Although—" he chuckled—"he insists you didn't do it alone—not three women. You had help from ghosts and fiends, who appeared from nowhere—and went back to nowhere."

"Ah, yes." Sybilla sighed faintly, her eyes wandered to the bowl of yellow roses on the table. "So few men know how to accept defeat gracefully."

*   *   *

They visited Ginny, while Sarah and Richard remained in the mews house to supervise Inga's packing. ("I'm afraid," Sybilla had murmured, "I don't trust her taking little ways.")

Ginny, too, had seemed brighter, like someone emerging from a spell. Life—however limited—was opening out before her again.

"I wish I could have been there." Raptly, Ginny listened to the carefully censored story. "And Inga really drank a bottle of glycerine and rosewater?" She gave the little wriggle of her eyebrows which ordinarily signalled a wriggle of her whole body. This time only her head moved.

"It's so exciting," she said. "Honestly, my toes are just curling with excitement—" She stopped abruptly, her eyes widening.

"You know," she said. "I think they are. I think they really are!"

Sybilla moved forward quickly and tossed back the bedclothes.

"Yes," Amy said shakily. "They really are."

"Then the motor impulses *are* all right." Sybilla replaced the blanket and stepped back.

"It will be a matter of therapy and exercise from now on," she said. "You needn't stay here for that. You can come north with us. Sarah can look after you, Amy will be able to help with the therapy. It will take time—but we'll have you on your feet again. You'll be walking by Christmas." It was more of an order than a statement.

"I guess I will." Ginny giggled hysterically. "I wouldn't dare not."

Inga's cases were in the hallway when they returned. There was going to be no delay about despatching her back to her Nordic wilderness. Although how long she might stay there, having seen the bright lights, was anybody's guess.

"I'll drive her to Harwich," Richard said, "and see her on to the boat for the Hook of Holland." There was obviously going to be no nonsense about depositing her at a main line station, with a long train journey ahead of her during which she might change her mind.

"I'll come along," Sarah said. "For the ride."

"A good idea," Sybilla agreed. She looked around the hallway carefully. "I believe I'll have this place redecorated while we're up North. I feel we can all do with a change."

The mink coat, torn and matted, huddled like a wounded animal on a chair. Sybilla eyed it with distaste. "I don't believe I'll ever want to wear *that* again," she said.

Inga's eyes began to gleam. She sidled nearer the mink.

"I'm not proud!" Sarah pounced on it gleefully. "Give it to me, Gran'mère. I don't mind wearing your cast-offs." She slipped it on, preening.

"I'll have it cleaned and mended for you," Sybilla said.

Inga tossed her head and moved away. "*I* vill have sable," she declared.

"Yes," Sybilla said drily. "You probably will."

"We'll be back soon," Richard spoke softly to Amy. "I'll see you then—there's a lot to talk about."

"All right." Amy admitted the beginning of a long and unending dialogue. "I'll be waiting here."

The following is a special preview collection from

THE WORLD OF MARIAN BABSON

MURDER ON A MYSTERY TOUR
When a real killer stalks a group of amateur sleuths on holiday, solving murders is no longer fun and games.

MURDER SAILS AT MIDNIGHT
Four wealthy women, sailing from New York to Genoa aboard the Italian luxury liner *Beatrice Cenci:* as the passengers frolic in the sumptuous elegance of her staterooms and cabarets, a killer stalks the decks under a full moon.

REEL MURDER
It's not easy to clear your name when it's a household word like Evangeline's—a silver screen queen of yesteryear. When the murders from her vintage screen plots are horrifyingly acted out, she could be next on the cutting-room floor.

MURDER, MURDER, LITTLE STAR
Little Twinkle—onscreen the brightest child star in filmdom, offscreen an insufferable brat who can get away with *anything*. In London to film *The Little Princess*, she's causing a sensation everywhere she goes—and making enemies. One of them might make this her last picture.

(ALL AVAILABLE FROM BANTAM BOOKS)

MURDER ON A MYSTERY TOUR

The knives were out at Chortlesby Manor.

Fish knives, butter knives, meat knives, carving knives, bread knives, fruit knives, even—in deference to the visitors expected soon—steak knives, were spread in glittering array across the pantry table.

An all-pervading smell of silver polish hung heavy in the air and the once-pristine butler's apron was grey-streaked and stained. The man wearing it gave a final vigorous rub to a pastry fork and set it down in the proper row. He frowned at it judiciously and picked it up again.

'Oh, let it be, Reggie,' his wife said from the doorway. 'If you get that silver any brighter, they'll have to wear dark glasses at the dinner table.'

'Steady on, old girl!' Reggie looked at her in alarm.

Midge sighed and ran her fingers through her hair. 'It's getting more difficult, though. It never seems to stop. I have to keep closing my eyes and thinking of our mortgage.'

'Hold on to that thought. Life may be more complicated these days, but it means we're climbing out of the red. Besides—' he beamed at her suddenly—it was the old Reggie grin, not the professional Mine Host smile he used so often these days. 'Besides—it's rather fun, isn't it?'

'Rather . . . We're certainly getting a different type of guest—not to mention a different sort of complaint.'

The sudden shrill peal of the bell startled them. With a clatter, a black and white card dropped into place in the rows of pigeonholes over the door. November 22 was at it again.

'Now *there's* someone I'd like to kill,' Midge said. 'I could cheerfully strangle her with my bare hands!' She started for the door.

'Yes, Mrs. Barbour—' Reggie waved a silencing hand as someone lifted the receiver at the other end of the line. 'Can we help you?'

'Ackroyd is in my room again.' Amaryllis Barbour's carrying voice scarcely needed the assistance of the telephone. 'He refuses to leave. I demand that you come up here and evict him!'

'I'll go up,' Midge said, as Reggie rubbed his ear.

'Ackroyd has a warped sense of humour,' Reggie said. 'He knows that woman hates him. He enjoys upsetting her.'

'Oh no.' Midge paused in the doorway, glaring. 'The *real* reason Ackroyd keeps stalking her is that he knows a big rat when he sees one!'

The thought cheered her all the way up the stairs and twitched the corners of her mouth as she tapped on the door.

'It took you long enough!' Mrs. Barbour appeared to believe that someone should materialize the instant she pulled her bell-rope. She stepped back, radiating fury and discontent.

'I'm sorry, Mrs. Barbour, we're very busy today.' Midge held on to her temper by visualizing a miniature Amaryllis Barbour clenched between Ackroyd's jaws, arms and legs dangling limply. 'The new guests are due in just a few hours.'

'I hope they're not going to disturb Bramwell,' Mrs. Barbour said severely. 'He is communing with his Muse. Nothing must be allowed to disrupt his train of thought.'

The clatter of a typewriter could be heard from the master bedroom opening off the sitting-room of the suite, bearing witness to Mrs. Barbour's remarks.

'I'm sure Bramwell will be able to finish his stint for the day in good time to welcome our guests and take part in the festivities.' Midge forced a smile.

'It is not a *stint*!' Amaryllis Barbour bristled. 'Genius knows no boundaries; nor is it ruled by hours. Bromwell does not "stint" his talent!'

Midge took a deep breath and reminded herself that it was nearly over. Just a few more days and she would never have to see either of the Barbours again. She allowed her mind to skip ahead to pleasanter considerations: as soon as they had left, she would disconnect the bell-pull and remove it. No future occupants of this suite would ever be able to demand her dancing attendance again. There were going to be some changes made, as well. When the new season started . . .

'I'll be glad to see the last of this nonsense.' Unwittingly, Amaryllis echoed Midge's thoughts. 'I simply cannot understand why Bramwell allowed himself to be roped into this charade in the first place.'

'You *have* had a nice holiday, haven't you?' Midge murmured gently. Six weeks in England, with all expenses paid, including free air flights, for only three weekends' work as Master of the Revels was pretty good going in anyone's language.

'Holiday? You call this a holiday? With poor Bramwell working his fingers to the bone?'

A fresh burst of machine-gun typing gave added impetus of her words.

'But I thought Bramwell was delighted that the book was going so well,' Midge said, as innocently as the vitriol dripping from her voice would allow. 'No one's forcing him to work on it. All he has to do is host three weekend parties. That isn't too arduous. Especially as he has Evelina T. Carterslee to act as hostess. She carries half the burden as Mistress of the Revels.'

'Bramwell should have been celebrity enough. I could quite easily have acted as his hostess. I always do at home.'

'It wasn't up to me,' Midge weaseled out from under the implied accusation. 'Death on Wheels and The Crimson Shroud organized everything from their end. Chortlesby Manor is just the venue.'

'*Miles* from the nearest town!'

'Only two miles. Some of the guests find it just a pleasant walk. In any case, there's always a car avail—'

'If you call *that* a car! I shall never understand how Bramwell allowed himself to be inveigled into this ridiculous enterprise. He should have had more sense. I don't know what he was thinking of!'

Midge made an indeterminate sound and looked around the sitting-room. Ackroyd was crouched beneath the television set, his baleful gaze fixed on Mrs. Barbour.

'And another thing—that creature! That Lettie—!'

Midge recognized that they were getting to the nub of Mrs. Barbour's complaints now. Ackroyd has simply been an excuse to acquire a listener.

'It's shameless, the way she's always in and out of the bedrooms—'

'Lettie has to go into all the bedrooms every night to turn down the covers. It's part of the routine.'

'That's no excuse. There's no need for her to keep going into Bramwell's. I can take care of that myself.' She sniffed. 'The way that female *flaunts* herself is disgraceful!'

No doubt about it, the old girl had her knife out for Lettie. Probably for any young pretty woman to whom her son was attracted. Not that she needed to worry. Lettie was not fool enough to tie herself up with a mother-in-law like that. Midge wondered how many times Amaryllis Barbour had ruined her son's chances. It could be no coincidence that he was nearing middle-age and still unmarried—not with mother constantly in tow.

'Come on, Ackroyd,' Midge called. There was no point in trying to argue with a brick wall. Amaryllis was Bramwell's problem—and he was welcome to her.

'And that cat should not be allowed to go into the guests' rooms.' Amaryllis was abruptly reminded of her original complaint. 'It's dangerous.'

'Oh, really!' Midge protested.

'It is! He could frighten someone into a heart attack. Or someone could trip over him. Not to mention people who might be allergic to—'

'Come on, Ackroyd.' Midge stooped and scooped him up before he could be blamed for the state of the economy, the attitude of the Common Market Commissioners and the next terrorist attack anywhere in the world. 'You're not wanted here.'

'He certainly isn't! There are too many creatures around this hotel pushing themselves in where they aren't wanted.'

Amaryllis Barbour took a deep breath and opened her mouth. Before she could launch into another Declaration, Midge, who had been quietly backing towards the door, slipped through it and closed it firmly behind her. She also closed her eyes and took a deep breath of her own.

From the corridor, the frantic typing was mercifully blurred. The loudest sound was Ackroyd's purr. Automatically, Midge ran her fingers through his white ruff and smoothed the long white streak of his chest. The purring grew louder. A rough little tongue dabbed at her finger.

Midge slumped weakly against the wall, eyes still closed, trying, as she had told Reggie, to think of the mortgage.

The sound of a doorknob turning brought her away from the wall and opened her eyes wide. Hugging Ackroyd defensively, she began edging away from Suite 22.

Straight into line with the door of Suite 21. The door swung wide and Evelina T. Carterslee stepped into the corridor.

'Having a spot of bother?' she asked sympathetically. She prided herself that she could pick up any local lingo in no time.

'Just a spot,' Midge said weakly. Through the open doorway, she could see Hermione and Cedric huddled over the table of tea-things. They were waving sheets of typescript at each other and it was obvious that an argument was developing.

'Thought so,' Evelina said triumphantly. 'You should have been warned. Bramwell isn't so bad, but no one in their right minds in the States would have allowed Sweet Amaryllis on the premises.'

'How were we to know?' Midge continued her crabwise progress toward the service stairs. 'We've only read the books. We don't know anything about your private lives.'

'Pity it couldn't have stayed that way, isn't it?' Evelina surveyed her with more than a trace of amusement breaking through her sympathy. 'Never mind, you'll know better next time.'

'Mmm.' Midge refrained from committing herself to any future prospects. She could not resist one question, however. 'Tell me, whatever happened to *Mr*. Barbour?'

'Rumour has it—' Evelina's eyes gleamed—'that Sweet Amaryllis ate him soon after mating!'

Ever one to recognize a good exit line, especially when she had uttered it herself, she stepped back into her suite and closed the door softly behind her.

Midge clawed weakly at the wallpapered panel that gave on to the service stairs. It swung open slightly and she stumbled through it, conscious of a great relief at escaping the rarefied atmosphere of Upstairs.

The knives were well and truly out at Chortlesby Manor.

MURDER SAILS AT MIDNIGHT

Butler had been one of the first on board. He liked it that way. It gave him time for an unhurried preliminary exploration of the layout. In the increasing flood of people pouring aboard, seeking cabin numbers, hunting farewell parties, he would not be noticed or remembered. That was the advantage of a nondescript face with no identifying marks.

Later, when the passengers themselves were settling down, he would move more cautiously to ascertain that the correct passenger was assigned to the cabin according to his information. Later still, when the passenger list was distributed on the second or third day out, he would make a final cross-check. He was meticulous on points like these. You didn't collect on the wrong body. And, on board ship, too many people didn't wind up in the same cabin they started out in. They imagined they were too near the engines, or the cooking smells, or that the ship would seem steadier from another location, and so they went running to the purser who, if at all possible, would find them alternative accommodation—purely for the sake of shutting them up, if for no other reason.

Meanwhile, the preliminary reconnaissance over, Butler stood in a shadowed hollow by a smokestack on the uppermost deck and looked down on the floodlit pier, watching the passengers come aboard.

The newspaper photograph had been blurred, but he thought he would recognize her when he saw her. Not that it was important to spot her in advance—they would be cast away together on this floating island for nearly a week, and she would not be able to escape—but it was a matter of pride to him that he do so.

Butler moved forward to the rail. Time was getting close. He looked down, both gangplanks were in view, a steady stream coming aboard. Overhead, cables creaked as cranes swung their loads of heavy crates up, over, and down into the cargo hold. Momentarily, he was diverted as he watched the longshoremen drive a neat little orange Fiat on to the loading platform and begin to secure the cables around it. Coals to Newcastle, you'd think.

Then he saw her. All other thoughts dissolved like the chimera they were. This was real. All his concentration burned down on that slight figure below. As though sensing something strange, she seemed to hesitate in her progress and raised her head.

Quickly, he stepped back into the shadows. He had seen enough. He frowned. More than enough—he hadn't been told about that. Just a little item the customer had forgotten to mention—or been ashamed to.

Butler lit another cigarette from the stub of the old one before pitching it over the side, watching the red arc of its descent, scattering fiery ashes as though to jettison its live tip before hitting the oily surface of the Hudson. This would take some thinking about.

It changed things. Not the basic fact—she was still his contract, and he prided himself on executing his contracts. But it made things different. Whether easier or harder remained to be seen. For one thing, it opened up a whole new era of weaknesses—a vulnerability which might be used against her when the time came.

Abruptly the public address system crackled into life with the first of the "All ashore" warnings. "Will all visitors kindly leave the ship . . . Will all visitors . . ." It was repeated in Italian. There was a high-pitched hum of consternation from the decks below him and a few of the more easily panicked began to fight their way down the gangplank against the still oncoming stream. The more experienced lingered, knowing that the announcement would be repeated at least twice more, at ten- or fifteen-minute intervals. There was no immediate hurry. For one thing, they were still loading cargo. Butler lit another cigarette . . .

One of the crew materialized suddenly near Butler, standing by to cast off the hawser looped over a stanchion. Butler froze, motionless. He had not been noticed.

Tugboats were getting up steam below, nuzzling up against the *Beatrice Cenci* fore and aft, ready to edge her away from the dock and out into the deep current of the river. They tooted and the deep commanding whistle of the *Beatrice Cenci* signalled back imperiously.

Passengers began lining the railing now, waving to those on shore. There was a gigantic creaking sigh as the gangplank was winched away from the ship, severing its frail connection with the land.

Suddenly, the *Beatrice Cenci* took on new life, riding high, dancing on tiptoe to break away, move out into her proper element. Again her whistle blasted, celebrating the removal of the last fetters binding her to the shore.

"*Good-bye* . . ." From the pier, they began throwing last kisses, shouting final frantic messages to those aboard. "*Don't forget to write* . . ."

Rippling, oil-slicked water gleamed in a widening triangle as the tugs nosed the prow of the *Beatrice Cenci* out into midstream, beginning to turn her, set her on her course.

"*Don't forget my Venetian glass* . . ."

The sailor slipped the lop off the stanchion, tossing it overboard. There was a sharp slap as it hit the water.

"*Take care* . . ." The cries from shore were fainter now, as though the criers were beginning to realize that they were fading away, blurring into the landscape, already faintly unreal.

Only the *Beatrice Cenci* was real now, throbbing into life, assuming her proper identity, becoming an entity in her own right.

"*Don't*—" One last message from shore rose above all the others in laughing urgency. "*Don't fall off the ship* . . ."

In the darkness, Butler smiled.

REEL MURDER

The cerise chiffon bows on my tap shoes kept coming undone and flapping all over the place. Busby Berkeley was furious with me. The rest of the chorus line was giggling and the star accused me of trying to upstage her.

"It won't do you any good," she snarled. "You'll just wind up on the cutting-room floor—where you belong!"

I was being my cutest, but it wasn't doing me any good. It was all a nightmare.

It was with relief that I heard the strange insistent noise summoning me back to consciousness and reality. I lay with open eyes staring into blackness while my mind caught up with me and told me that I was in England and the odd *brrr-brrr* noise that wouldn't stop was the telephone on my bedside table. I groped for it, knocking something unidentifiable off the table—I hoped it wasn't the lamp.

"Yes, yes. I mean, hello. Who is it—?" I groped again, this time connecting with the lamp and switched it on. "Who—?" I blinked, covering my eyes against the sudden brightness.

"Who is it?" another voice demanded. It wasn't mine. "Do you realize what time it is?" I recognized Evangeline's indignant tones.

"Get off the line!" Another indignant voice snarled back at her. "I'm calling my mother. What are you doing answering?"

"Martha—" I groaned, finally identifying the distant voice. "Why are you calling at this hour?" I blinked at my watch and it swam into reluctant focus. "It's four o'clock in the morning. What's the matter? What's wrong?"

"Matter?" she wailed. "Wrong? That's what I want to know. You never called me. Did the plane land safely? Are you all right?"

"Don't be absurd!" Evangeline snapped from her extension. "If anything had happened to that plane, you'd have heard about it. It would have made headlines all over the world."

"But anything could have happened after you landed. There could have been an automobile accident—"

"Nonsense," I said quickly, before Evangeline could. "Hugh is a very careful driver. We were perfectly safe."

"Hugh? Who's Hugh?"

"Hugh," Evangeline said icily, through clenched teeth, "is an English gigolo who swept your mother off her feet the moment she arrived. I had to forcibly remove him from her bedroom just a few hours ago. All your worst fears are realized. If you value your inheritance, you will rush over and join me in the unequal struggle to keep your lust-ridden mother from the arms of this fortune-hunting monster."

"Mother!" Martha wailed. "Mother—!"

"Mother—!"

"Evangeline—get off the line! This is my call!"

"I'll do my best, Martha, but you know your mother. There are times when there's just no holding her."

"Mother—!"

"Evangeline—hang up!"

"You mustn't blame her, Martha. It's just the way she's made. *Made* being the operative word, of course."

"Mother—!"

"Evangeline, I'm going to kill you!" At last, I was awake enough to realize the futility of shouting into a telephone when two raving egomaniacs were on the line. I set down the receiver on the bedside table, shuffled into my slippers and went across the hall into Evangeline's room.

"All right, that's enough!" I slammed my fingers down on the telephone cradle, cutting her off. "You ought to know better! How dare you upset Martha like that? You know she's a bit naïve?"

"Naïve?" Evangeline snorted. "Face it, Trixie—you're seventy-five years old and your only daughter is a gibbering middle-aged idiot!"

"I'm only sixty-eight," I said coldly. "And Martha is forty. That's hardly middle-aged these days. Besides, she means well. She has my best interests at heart."

"Hmmph!" Evangeline settled back against the pillows. "You should have beaten her more when she was a child."

"If I had, she'd probably be writing a book about it now."

"She may be doing that anyway."

"You should talk! You're old enough to have outgrown the mischief-making stage. You must be eighty now—or is it eight-five?"

"I haven't decided recently," Evangeline said thoughtfully. "Which do you think is more effective? Or maybe I should stick at seventy-six for a few more years?"

I snorted in my turn and stormed back to my own bedroom. The telephone was still projecting strange ululating noises. I picked it up carefully and held it to my ear.

"Mother—" Martha wailed. "Mother—speak to me!"

"Oh, shut up!" I snarled and slammed down the receiver.

My second awakening was more peaceful. There was no sound from Evageline's room and the clock told me it was ten a.m. With luck, I might have some time to myself before she awoke. I rose and went into the kitchen to put the kettle on.

A woolly white cloud seemed pressed against every window. When I got closer to a window, the cloud receded a bit and I was able to look out into a hazy landscape. What a waste to have a setting like that and no camera to capture it, no actors to begin the promised drama.

Abruptly, I remembered just what it was like to be acting out-of-doors on location in a setting like that: the damp chill creeping into your bones while you waited for the dozens of technicians to arrange and rearrange their bits; the endless retakes while you grew colder and wetter, until your fingers were too numb to hold the props and your brain too numb to remember the dialogue. No, the garden could remain an empty setting, a lost location, for all I cared now. Those days were long behind me. I hadn't thought of them in years.

The kettle began whistling shrilly and I rushed to turn it off before it woke Evangeline.

"Hmmmph!" Too late. She made one of her Entrances—so she was in that mood today—drawing her heavy black velvet robe closer around her and doing up the gold braid frogs and clinching her waist (still a trim one) with the heavy gold cord.

"Good morning, Evangeline." She made me feel like a frump in my quilted glazed cotton housecoat—so carefully chosen for me by Martha last Mother's Day.

Evangeline seated herself at the tiny table and looked around fretfully. When I didn't move, she got up again, found herself a cup and saucer, the jar of instant coffee and made her own coffee.

"Toast?" I asked as the toaster popped; there were two slices in there anyway.

"Oh, all right," she said, doing me a favour.

Evangeline munched absently, looking out at the fog-shrouded garden, thinking her own thoughts.

"The garden must have been lovely in the summer." I said. "It's sort of pretty and atmospheric now—in a spooky kind of way."

"Spooky is right," Evangeline frowned out at the fog. "It looks like a good place to bury a body."

"Trust you to think of that!"

"What's that?" There had been a sharp metallic click from somewhere at the front of the flat. My nerves weren't as on edge as Evangeline's appeared to be, but we both went to investigate.

At the end of the tiny vetisbule, two square white envelopes lay just inside the door beneath an oblong slot in the door that I had not noticed last night.

"It's just the mail," I said thankfully. I didn't feel strong enough to cope with anything more vital. From the hallway outside, we heard the front door close firmly.

I stooped and gathered up the envelopes while Evangeline went on into the drawing-room. There was one for each of us, but I noticed there was no stamp or franking on the envelopes. They had been delivered by hand, then; presumably by the person who had just left.

Evangeline was standing at one of the drawing-room windows, looking out at the circular carriageway. I joined her just in time to see a tall dark shape walk into the mist at the end of the carriageway and disappear on the other side of the wall that bordered the property.

Heavy footsteps thundered down the hall stairs from the top floor, paused at the landing above, then descended more slowly and quietly. Someone had obviously taken sudden thought of the two elderly ladies in the ground-floor flat.

Again the front door closed quietly and a figure stood on the top step squinting into the fog.

"Who's that?" Evangeline frowned. "How many people do they have living in that top flat, anyway? It must be crowded."

"I think . . . Yes, it is. It's Des, but he's done something to his hair."

'He must have. He looks quite normal."

"Crestfallen, in fact." He had washed the multicolours out of his hair and his spikes had been flattened down to a rather uneven, but unremarkable style. "So that's what they do with it when they want to go out to work." He was carrying a clarinet case and would not now look out of place in an orchestra.

"He's the sensible one. There's not much that other boy c⌐ ⌐o about his Mohican cut—except wait for all the shaved parts to grow back."

"Ah, the Indian scalplock!" Evangeline sighed reminiscently. "I haven't seen a style like that since *The Revenge of the White Squaw*. How it takes me back. Now, *that* was a picture!"

"They don't make them like that any more," I agreed. They wouldn't dare. The title alone would make it impossibly racist and sexist today. I wondered whether they would be showing it in the Retrospective or whether all that violence would rule it out. I'd heard the English were more sensitive than we were to things like that."

"Well," Evangeline said brusquely. 'Are you going to stand around mooning all day, or are you going to give me my letter? Our marching orders, I'll be bound. We might as well know the worst."

"Oh, it's not so bad—" I tore open the envelope and scanned the brief lines. "Lunch with Beauregard Sylvester at the Ivy at one. I presume yours is the same. A car will call to collect us."

"Lunch . . . with Beauregard Sylvester . . ." Evangeline made it sound like a date with the tumbrils. "I do believe I'm getting one of my splitting headaches. You'll have to go without me."

"Oh no you don't!" She wasn't going to start getting away with that again. "He was *your* co-star in all those pictures. You're going to have to meet him sometime. You can have a couple of aspirins and lie down for a while—but we're both going to that lunch!"

MURDER, MURDER, LITTLE STAR

Heathrow, by dawn's early light, was a futuristic city peopled by ghosts obviously regretting their past lives, especially the one they had last night. Frances parked the car and marched purposefully past grey-faced automatons who were carrying, wheeling or just slumped over pieces of luggage.

"Over here!" Mr. Herkimer hailed her and waved her onwards. "We want Gate 12—that's where our Red-eye Flight comes in."

Racing across the terminal with Mr. Herkimer, already slightly out of breath, Frances became aware of an unnerving swishing sound following after them. She turned to see two uniformed attendants scurrying behind them, pushing empty wheelchairs. They increased their speed when Mr. Herkimer increased his speed, swerved when he swerved, slowed when he slowed. There was no escaping them; they were definitely with Mr. Herkimer. For the first time, Frances was conscious of a feeling of foreboding.

"This way!" He snatched at her elbow and propelled her along. "We've got permission to go straight through. On accounta *them*." He jerked his thumb backwards and when Frances turned around, she saw that several reporters and cameramen had joined the wheelchair men, leaving her uncertain which ones Mr. Herkimer was referring to.

"Mr.—Herkie—" She plucked at his sleeve. "Is there anything wrong?" She had a sudden vision of a heap of crumpled wreckage on a runway. "Has something happened?"

"You mean *them*?" He shook his head. "Naw, that's okay. They're just here to take Morris to the ambulance."

"Ambulance?"

"Take it easy, will you?" He slowed a little, going through the gate. "I told you there's nothing wrong. It's only Morris. Morris Moskva—greatest scriptwriter your ever saw, but he can't stand planes. Morris hasn't made a vertical flight in twenty years. He figures, if the plane crashes, he don't want to know about it. So we wheel him on at one end and wheel him off at the other. Then we just throw him on a bed in the hotel until he sleeps off the pills. After that, he's ready to work. Greatest scriptwriter you ever saw—when he's conscious, that is."

"Yes, but—" Frances was only partly mollified. "But does it take *two* wheelchairs to carry him?"

"Well, I'll tell you. Sometimes Laurenda isn't always feeling so good. Twinkle's mother, you know? So the second wheelchair is a sort of back-up operation. Just in case she needs it."

"I see," Frances said. Her uneasiness increased.

"Here you are—" The Immigration Officer was just finishing, he extended a slim grey passport to the overdressed midget. "Welcome to England Miss Tilling—"

"What was that name—?" one of the newsmen began.

"Twinkle!" Mr. Herkimer swooped on the midget, enveloping her in an embrace she did not appear to relish. "This is Twinkle—our ten-year-old star. Twinkle—that's the only name she's got. Twinkle—like in star."

"This is our Frances—" Mr. Herkimer contrived to kiss Laurenda Tilling on one cheek, introduce Frances, pat Twinkle on the head, wave the stewardess beyond the Immigration barrier and direct one wheelchair plus attendant towards the plane—all at the same moment. "Frances Armitage. I promise you, Laurenda, she's a doll. You won't have a problem in the world while she's around. She'll take care of everything."

Laurenda Tilling waved a limp hand in her direction. Twinkle ignored her. The stewardess advanced mechanically and began unloading her burdens into Frances's unresisting arms.

Flashbulbs were popping off all around them. Blinking through an after-image of coloured flashes, Frances saw Twinkle round on a photographer who had been staring at her.

"What's the matter?" Twinkle demanded. "Haven't you ever seen sable before?"

"Not on anyone under forty," the photographer mumbled.

"Twinkle, darling—" Mr. Herkimer, too, had heard the exchange and swooped on her. He pressed her to his capacious abdomen, one hand covering her mouth, and patted her head again with his other hand.

"Such a long journey—" he said to the journalists—"for such a little girl. She's tired, but she's delighted to be here in London and looking forward to making this film with the cream of the English theatre as her co-stars—ouch!"

"Supporting players," Twinkle said coldly. Mr. Herkimer was nursing his hand, on which a semicircle of sharp indentations was clearly visible.

"Jet lag!" Mr. Herkimer burst in. "She's only ten years old and she's exhausted. It's been an all-night flight, remember. Later on, we'll call a Press Conference. She'll answer all your questions then."

The stewardess finished transferring her burdens and looked at Frances curiously. "You're actually joining this circus?" she asked.

"I've already joined," Frances said

The wheelchair swished past on its return journey, a massive shape huddled in it, swathed in a rumpled blanket.

"Here!" The sight seemed to inspire Mr. Herkimer. "Over here!" He beckoned frantically to the second wheelchair and attendant.

Silently, Frances and the stewardess watched as Laurenda Tilling sank into the wheelchair, eyes closed, looking paler than ever. Twinkle, the limelight abruptly wrenched away from her, hovered in the background, abruptly looking as unhappy and miserable as any ten-year-old whose mother was on the verge of inexplicable collapse.

Instinctively, Frances moved forward.

"Here—" The stewardess pushed a small vial of capsules at her. "You'd better take these. You're going to need them. It's all right," she added, as she saw the uneasy expression flit across Frances's face. "They're only tranquillizers."

"But—" Frances felt her fingers close over the vial as though it were a straw and she were drowning. "Who are they for?" She looked from one wheelchair to the other, to Twinkle, even to Mr. Herkimer.

"Are you kidding?" The stewardess patted her hand and began to edge away, relief emanating from every fibre of her being. "They're for *you*. Who else? Believe me, dearie, you're gonna need them!"

ABOUT THE AUTHOR

MARIAN BABSON is the author of more than twenty-five mysteries. Winner of the Poisoned Chalice and Sleuth awards, she was also a nominee for the British Gold and Silver Dagger awards. She is listed in *Publishers Weekly* as one of today's best British mystery writers. She lives in London.

BANTAM MYSTERY COLLECTION